Defender of the INNOCENT:

THE CASEBOOK OF MARTIN EHRENGRAF

Defender of the INNOCENT:

THE CASEBOOK OF MARTIN EHRENGRAF

LAWRENCE BLOCK

SUBTERRANEAN PRESS 2014

Defender of the Innocent: the Casebook of Martin Ehrengraf

First Subterranean Press Edition

ISBN
978-1-59606-667-0

Subterranean Press
PO Box 190106
Burton, MI 48519

subterraneanpress.com

TABLE OF CONTENTS

The EHRENGRAF Defense

"Can storied urn or animated bust
Back to its mansion call the fleeting breath?
Can Honour's voice provoke the silent dust,
Or Flattery sooth the dull cold ear of death?"
—Thomas Gray

Mrs. Culhane," Martin Ehrengraf said. "Do sit down, yes, I think you will find that chair comfortable. And please pardon the disarray. It is the natural condition of my office. Chaos stimulates me. Order stifles me. It is absurd, is it not, but so then is life itself, eh?"

Dorothy Culhane sat, nodded. She studied the small, trimly built man who remained standing behind his extremely disorderly desk. Her eyes took in the narrow mustache, the thin lips, the deeply set dark eyes. If the man liked clutter in his surroundings, he certainly made up for it in his grooming and attire. He wore a starched white shirt, a perfectly tailored dove gray three-button suit, a narrow dark blue necktie.

Oh, but she did not want to think about neckties—

"Of course you are Clark Culhane's mother," Ehrengraf said. "I had it that you had already retained an attorney."

"Alan Farrell."

"A good man," Ehrengraf said. "An excellent reputation."

"I dismissed him this morning."

"Ah."

Mrs. Culhane took a deep breath. "He wanted Clark to plead guilty," she said. "Temporary insanity, something of the sort. He wanted my son to admit to killing that girl."

"And you did not wish him to do this."

"My son is innocent!" The words came in a rush, uncontrollably. She calmed herself. "My son is innocent," she repeated, levelly now. "He could never kill anyone. He can't admit to a crime he never committed in the first place."

"And when you said as much to Farrell—"

"He told me he was doubtful of his ability to conduct a successful defense based on a plea of innocent." She drew herself up. "So I decided to find someone who could."

"And you came to me."

"Yes."

The little lawyer had seated himself. Now he was doodling on a lined yellow scratch pad. "Do you know much about me, Mrs. Culhane?"

"Not very much. It's said that your methods are unorthodox."

"Indeed."

"But that you get results."

"Results. Indeed, results." Martin Ehrengraf made a tent of his fingertips and, for the first time since she had entered his office, a smile bloomed briefly on his thin lips. "Indeed I get results. I must get results, my dear Mrs. Culhane, or else I do not get my dinner. And while my slimness might indicate otherwise, it is my custom to eat very well indeed. You see, I do something which no other criminal lawyer does, at least not to my knowledge. You have heard what this is?"

"I understand you operate on a contingency basis."

"A contingency basis." Ehrengraf was nodding emphatically. "Yes, that is precisely what I do. I operate on a contingency basis. My fees are high, Mrs. Culhane. They are extremely high. But they are due and payable only in the event that my efforts are crowned with success. If a client of mine is found guilty, then my work on his behalf costs him nothing."

The lawyer got to his feet again, stepped out from behind his desk. Light glinted on his highly polished black shoes. "This is common enough in negligence cases. The attorney gets a share in the settlement. If he loses he gets nothing. How much greater is his incentive to perform to the best of his ability, eh? But why limit this practice to negligence suits? Why not have all lawyers paid in this fashion? And doctors, for that matter. If the operation's a failure, why not let the doctor absorb some of the loss, eh? But such an arrangement would be a long time coming, I am afraid. Yet I have found it workable in my practice. And my clients have been pleased by the results."

"If you can get Clark acquitted—"

"Acquitted?" Ehrengraf rubbed his hands together. "Mrs. Culhane, in my most notable successes it is not even a question of acquittal. It is rather a matter of the case never even coming to trial. New evidence is discovered, the actual miscreant confesses or is brought to justice, and one way or another charges against my client are dropped. Courtroom pyrotechnics, wizardry in cross-examination—ah, I prefer to leave that to the Perry Masons of the world. It is not unfair to say, Mrs. Culhane, that I am more the detective than the lawyer. What is the saying? 'The best defense is a good offense.' Or perhaps it is the other way around, the best offense being a good defense, but it hardly matters. It is a saying in warfare and in the game of chess, I believe, and neither serves as the ideal metaphor for what concerns us. And what does concern us, Mrs. Culhane—" and he leaned toward her and the dark eyes flashed "—what concerns us is saving your son's life and securing his freedom and preserving his reputation. Yes?"

"Yes. Yes, of course."

"The evidence against your son is considerable, Mrs. Culhane. The dead girl, Althea, was his former fiancée. It is said that she jilted him—"

"He broke the engagement."

"I don't doubt that for a moment, but the prosecution would have it otherwise. This girl was strangled. Around her throat was found a necktie."

Mrs. Culhane's eyes went involuntarily to the lawyer's own blue tie, then slipped away.

"A particular necktie, Mrs. Culhane. A necktie made exclusively for and worn exclusively by members of the Caedmon Society at Oxford

University. Your son attended Dartmouth, Mrs. Culhane, and after graduation he spent a year in advanced study in England."

"Yes."

"At Oxford University."

"Yes."

"Where he became a member of the Caedmon Society."

"Yes."

Ehrengraf breathed in through clenched teeth. "He owned a necktie of the Caedmon Society. He appears to be the only member of the society residing in this city and would thus presumably be the only person to own such a tie. He cannot produce that tie, nor can he provide a satisfactory alibi for the night in question."

"Someone must have stolen his tie."

"The murderer, of course."

"To frame him."

"Of course," Ehrengraf said soothingly. "There could be no other explanation, could there?" He breathed in, he breathed out, he set his chin decisively. "I will undertake your son's defense," he announced. "And on my usual terms."

"Oh, thank heavens."

"My fee will be seventy-five thousand dollars. That is a great deal of money, Mrs. Culhane, although you might very well have ended up paying Mr. Farrell that much or more by the time you'd gone through the tortuous processes of trial and appeal and so on, and after he'd presented an itemized accounting of his expenses. My fee includes any and all expenses which I might incur. No matter how much time and effort and money I spend on your son's behalf, the cost to you will be limited to the figure I named. And none of that will be payable unless your son is freed. Does that meet with your approval?"

She hardly had to hesitate but made herself take a moment before replying. "Yes," she said. "Yes, of course. The terms are satisfactory."

"Another point. If, ten minutes from now, the district attorney should decide of his own accord to drop all charges against your son, you nevertheless owe me seventy-five thousand dollars. Even though I should have done nothing to earn it."

"I don't see—"

The thin lips smiled. The dark eyes did not participate in the smile. "It is my policy, Mrs. Culhane. Most of my work, as I have said, is more the work of a detective than the work of a lawyer. I operate largely behind the scenes and in the shadows. Perhaps I set currents in motion. Often when the smoke clears it is hard to prove to what extent my client's victory is the fruit of my labor. I do not attempt to prove anything of the sort. I merely share in the victory by collecting my fee in full whether I seem to have earned it or not. You understand?"

It did seem reasonable, even if the explanation was the slightest bit hazy. Perhaps the little man dabbled in bribery, perhaps he knew the right strings to pull but could scarcely disclose them after the fact. Well, it hardly mattered. All that mattered was Clark's freedom, Clark's good name.

"Yes," she said. "Yes, I understand. When Clark is released you'll be paid in full."

"Very good."

She frowned. "In the meantime you'll want a retainer, won't you? An advance of some sort?"

"You have a dollar?" She looked in her purse, drew out a dollar bill. "Give it to me, Mrs. Culhane. Very good, very good. An advance of one dollar against a fee of seventy-five thousand dollars. And I assure you, my dear Mrs. Culhane, that should this case not resolve itself in unqualified success I shall even return this dollar to you." The smile, and this time there was a twinkle in the eyes. "But that will not happen, Mrs. Culhane, because I do not intend to fail."

It was a little more than a month later when Dorothy Culhane made her second visit to Martin Ehrengraf's office. This time the little lawyer's suit was a navy blue pinstripe, his necktie maroon with a subdued below-the-knot design. His starched white shirt might have been the same one she had seen on her earlier visit. The shoes, black wing tips, were as highly polished as the other pair he'd been wearing.

His expression was changed slightly. There was something that might have been sorrow in the deep-set eyes, a look that suggested a continuing disappointment with human nature.

"It would seem quite clear," Ehrengraf said now. "Your son has been released. All charges have been dropped. He is a free man, free even to the extent that no shadow of suspicion hangs over him in the public mind."

"Yes," Mrs. Culhane said, "and that's wonderful, and I couldn't be happier about it. Of course it's terrible about the girls, I hate to think that Clark's happiness and my own happiness stem from their tragedy, or I suppose it's tragedies, isn't it, but all the same I feel—"

"Mrs. Culhane."

She bit off her words, let her eyes meet his.

"Mrs. Culhane, it's quite cut and dried, is it not? You owe me seventy-five thousand dollars."

"But—"

"We discussed this, Mrs. Culhane. I'm sure you recall our discussion. We went over the matter at length. Upon the successful resolution of this matter you were to pay me my fee, seventy-five thousand dollars. Less, of course, the sum of one dollar already paid over to me as a retainer."

"But—"

"Even if I did nothing. Even if the district attorney elected to drop charges before you'd even departed from these premises. That, I believe, was the example I gave at the time."

"Yes."

"And you agreed to those terms."

"Yes, but—"

"But what, Mrs. Culhane?"

She took a deep breath, set herself bravely. "Three girls," she said. "Strangled, all of them, just like Althea Patton. All of them the same physical type, slender blondes with high foreheads and prominent front teeth, two of them here in town and one across the river in Montclair, and around each of their throats—"

"A necktie."

"The same necktie."

"A necktie of the Caedmon Society of Oxford University."

"Yes." She drew another breath. "So it was obvious that there's a maniac at large," she went on, "and the last killing was in Montclair, so maybe he's leaving the area, and my God, I hope so, it's terrifying, the idea of a man just killing girls at random because they remind him of his mother—"

"I beg your pardon?"

"That's what somebody was saying on television last night. A psychiatrist. It was just a theory."

"Yes," Ehrengraf said. "Theories are interesting, aren't they? Speculation, guesswork, hypotheses, all very interesting."

"But the point is—"

"Yes?"

"I know what we agreed, Mr. Ehrengraf. I know all that. But on the other hand you made one visit to Clark in prison, that was just one brief visit, and then as far as I can see you did nothing at all, and just because the madman happened to strike again and killed the other girls in exactly the same manner and even used the same tie, well, you have to admit that seventy-five thousand dollars sounds like quite a windfall for you."

"A windfall."

"So I was discussing this with my own attorney—he's not a criminal lawyer, he handles my personal affairs—and he suggested that you might accept a reduced fee as way of settlement."

"He suggested this, eh?"

She avoided the man's eyes. "Yes, he did suggest it, and I must say it seems reasonable to me. Of course I would be glad to reimburse you for any expenses you incurred, although I can't honestly say that you could have run up much in the way of expenses, and he suggested that I might give you a fee on top of that of five thousand dollars, but I am grateful, Mr. Ehrengraf, and I'd be willing to make that *ten* thousand dollars, and you have to admit that's not a trifle, don't you? I have money, I'm comfortably set up financially, but no one can afford to pay out seventy-five thousand dollars for nothing at all, and—"

"Human beings," Ehrengraf said, and closed his eyes. "And the rich are the worst of all," he added, opening his eyes, fixing them upon Dorothy Culhane. "It is an unfortunate fact of life that only the rich can afford to pay high fees. Thus I must make my living acting on their behalf. The poor, they do not agree to an arrangement when they are desperate and go back on their word when they are in more reassuring circumstances."

"It's not so much that I'd go back on my word," Mrs. Culhane said. "It's just that—"

"Mrs. Culhane."

"Yes?"

"I am going to tell you something which I doubt will have any effect upon you, but at least I shall have tried. The best thing you could do, right at this moment, would be to take out your checkbook and write out a check to me for payment in full. You will probably not do this, and you will ultimately regret it."

"Is that...are you threatening me?"

A flicker of a smile. "Certainly not. I have given you not a threat but a prediction. You see, if you do not pay my fee, what I shall do is tell you something else which will lead you to pay me my fee after all."

"I don't understand."

"No," Martin Ehrengraf said. "No, I don't suppose you do. Mrs. Culhane, you spoke of expenses. You doubted I could have incurred significant expenses on your son's behalf. There are many things I could say, Mrs. Culhane, but I think it might be best for me to confine myself to a brisk accounting of a small portion of my expenses."

"I don't—"

"Please, my dear lady. Expenses. If I were listing my expenses, dear lady, I would begin by jotting down my train fare to New York City. Then taxi fare to Kennedy Airport, which comes to twenty dollars with tip and bridge tolls, and isn't that exorbitant?"

"Mr. Ehrengraf—"

"Please. Then airfare to London and back. I always fly first class, it's an indulgence, but since I pay my own expenses out of my own pocket I feel I have the right to indulge myself. Next a rental car hired from Heathrow Airport and driven to Oxford and back. The price of gasoline is high enough over here, Mrs. Culhane, but in England they call it petrol and charge the earth for it."

She stared at him. His hands were folded atop his disorderly desk and he went on talking in the calmest possible tone of voice and she felt her jaw dropping but could not seem to raise it back into place.

"In Oxford I had to visit five gentlemen's clothiers, Mrs. Culhane. One shop had no Caedmon Society cravats in stock at the moment. I purchased one necktie from each of the other shops. I felt it really wouldn't do to buy more than one tie in any one shop. A man prefers not to call attention to himself unnecessarily. The Caedmon Society necktie, Mrs. Culhane, is not unattractive. A navy blue field with a half-inch stripe of royal blue and two narrower flanking stripes, one of gold and the other of a rather bright green. I don't care for regimental stripes myself, Mrs. Culhane, preferring as I do a more subdued style in neckwear, but the Caedmon tie is a handsome one all the same."

"My God."

"There were other expenses, Mrs. Culhane, but as I pay them myself I don't honestly think there's any need for me to recount them to you, do you?"

"My God. Dear God in heaven."

"Indeed. It would have been better all around, as I said a few moments ago, had you decided to pay my fee without hearing what you've just heard. Ignorance in this case would have been, if not bliss, at least a good deal closer to bliss than what you're undoubtedly feeling at the moment."

"Clark didn't kill that girl."

"Of course he didn't, Mrs. Culhane. Of course he didn't. I'm sure some rotter stole his tie and framed him. But that would have been an enormous chore to prove and all a lawyer could have done was persuade a jury that there was room for doubt, and poor Clark would have had a cloud over him all the days of his life. Of course you and I know he's innocent—"

"He *is* innocent," she said. "He *is.*"

"Of course he is, Mrs. Culhane. The killer was a homicidal maniac striking down young women who reminded him of his mother. Or his sister, or God knows whom. You'll want to get out your checkbook, Mrs. Culhane, but don't try to write the check just yet. Your hands are trembling. Just sit there, that's the ticket, and I'll get you a glass of water. Everything's perfectly fine, Mrs. Culhane. That's what you must remember. Everything's perfectly fine and everything will continue to be fine. Here you are, a couple of ounces of water in a paper cup, just drink it down, there you are, there you are."

And when it was time to write out the check her hand did not shake a bit. Pay to the order of Martin H. Ehrengraf, seventy-five thousand dollars, signed Dorothy Rodgers Culhane. Signed with a ball-point pen, no need to blot it, and handed across the desk to the impeccably dressed little man.

"Yes, thank you, thank you very much, my dear lady. And here is your dollar, the retainer you gave me. Go ahead and take it, please."

She took the dollar.

"Very good. And you probably won't want to repeat this conversation to anyone. What would be the point?"

"No. No, I won't say anything."

"Of course not."

"Four neckties."

He looked at her, raised his eyebrows a fraction of an inch.

"You said you bought four of the neckties. There were—there were three girls killed."

"Indeed there were."

"What happened to the fourth necktie?"

"Why, it must be in my bureau drawer, don't you suppose? And perhaps they're all there, Mrs. Culhane. Perhaps all four neckties are in my bureau drawer, still in their original wrappings, and purchasing them was just a waste of time and money on my part. Perhaps that homicidal maniac had neckties of his own and the four in my drawer are just an interesting souvenir and a reminder of what might have been."

"Oh."

"And perhaps I've just told you a story out of the whole cloth, an interesting turn of phrase since we are speaking of silk neckties. Perhaps I never flew to London at all, never motored to Oxford, never purchased a single necktie of the Caedmon Society. Perhaps that was just something I trumped up on the spur of the moment to coax a fee out of you."

"But—"

"Ah, my dear lady," said Ehrengraf, moving to the side of her chair, taking her arm, helping her out of the chair, turning her, steering her toward the door. "We would do well, Mrs. Culhane, to believe that which it most pleases us to believe. I have my fee. You have your son. The police have another line of inquiry to pursue altogether. It would seem we've all come out of this well, wouldn't you say? Put your mind at rest, Mrs. Culhane, dear Mrs. Culhane. There's the elevator down the hall on your left. If you ever need my services you know where I am and how to reach me. And perhaps recommend me to your friends. But discreetly, dear lady. Discreetly. Discretion is everything in matters of this sort."

Mrs. Culhane walked very carefully down the hall to the elevator and rang the bell and waited. And she did not look back. Not once.

The EHRENGRAF Presumption

"Ill fares the land, to hastening ills a prey,
Where wealth accumulates and men decay."
—Oliver Goldsmith

"Now let me get this straight," Alvin Gort said. "You actually accept criminal cases on a contingency basis. Even homicide cases?"

"Especially homicide cases."

"If your client is acquitted he pays your fee. If he's found guilty, then your efforts on his behalf cost him nothing whatsoever. Except expenses, I assume."

"That's very true," Martin Ehrengraf said. The little lawyer supplied a smile which blossomed briefly on his thin lips while leaving his eyes quite uninvolved. "Shall I explain in detail?"

"By all means."

"To take your last point first, I pay my own expenses and furnish no accounting of them to my client. My fees are thus all-inclusive. By the same token, should a client of mine be convicted he would owe me nothing. I would absorb such expenses as I might incur acting on his behalf."

"That's remarkable."

"It's surely unusual, if not unique. Now the rest of what you've said is essentially true. It's not uncommon for attorneys to take on negligence cases on a contingency basis, participating handsomely in the settlement when they win, sharing their clients' losses when they do not. The principle has always made eminent good sense to me. Why shouldn't a client give substantial value for value received? Why should he be simply charged for service, whether or not the service does him any good? When I pay out money, Mr. Gort, I like to get what I pay for. And I don't mind paying for what I get."

"It certainly makes sense to me," Alvin Gort said. He dug a cigarette from a pack in his shirt pocket, scratched a match, drew smoke into his lungs. This was his first experience in a jail cell and he'd been quite surprised to learn that he was allowed to have matches on his person, to wear his own clothes rather than prison garb, to keep money in his pocket and a watch on his wrist.

No doubt all this would change if and when he were convicted of murdering his wife. Then he'd be in an actual prison and the rules would most likely be more severe. Here they had taken his belt as a precaution against suicide, and they would have taken the laces from his shoes had he not been wearing loafers at the time of his arrest. But it could have been worse.

And unless Ehrengraf pulled off a small miracle, it would be worse.

"Sometimes my clients never see the inside of a courtroom," Ehrengraf was saying now. "I'm always happiest when I can save them not merely from prison but from going to trial in the first place. So you should understand that whether or not I collect my fee hinges on your fate, on the disposition of your case—and not on how much work I put in or how much time it takes me to liberate you. In other words, from the moment you retain me I have an interest in your future, and the moment you are released and all charges dropped, my fee becomes due and payable in full."

"And your fee will be—?"

"One hundred thousand dollars," Ehrengraf said crisply.

Alvin Gort considered the sum, then nodded thoughtfully. It was not difficult to believe that the diminutive attorney commanded and received large fees. Alvin Gort recognized good clothing when he saw it, and the clothing Martin Ehrengraf wore was good indeed. The man was well turned out. His suit, a bronze sharkskin number with a nipped-in waist, was clearly not off the rack. His brown wing-tip shoes had been polished to a high gloss. His tie, a rich teak in hue with an unobtrusive below-the-knot design, bore the reasonably discreet trademark of a genuine countess. And his hair had received the attention of a good barber while his neatly trimmed mustache served as a focal point for a face otherwise devoid of any single dominating feature. The overall impression thus created was one of a man who could announce a six-figure fee and make you feel that such a sum was altogether fitting and proper.

"I'm reasonably well off," Gort said.

"I know. It's a commendable quality in clients."

"And I'd certainly be glad to pay one hundred thousand dollars for my freedom. On the other hand, if you don't get me off then I don't owe you a dime. Is that right?"

"Quite right."

Gort considered again, nodded again. "Then I've got no reservations," he said. "But—"

"Yes?"

Alvin Gort's eyes measured the lawyer. Gort was accustomed to making rapid decisions. He made one now.

"You might have reservations," he said. "There's one problem."

"Oh?"

"I did it," Gort said. "I killed her."

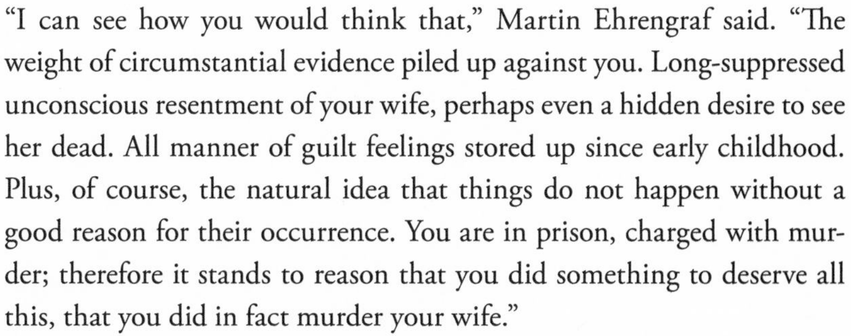

"I can see how you would think that," Martin Ehrengraf said. "The weight of circumstantial evidence piled up against you. Long-suppressed unconscious resentment of your wife, perhaps even a hidden desire to see her dead. All manner of guilt feelings stored up since early childhood. Plus, of course, the natural idea that things do not happen without a good reason for their occurrence. You are in prison, charged with murder; therefore it stands to reason that you did something to deserve all this, that you did in fact murder your wife."

"But I did," Gort said.

"Nonsense. Palpable nonsense."

"But I was there," Gort said. "I'm not making this up. For God's sake, man, I'm not a psychiatric basket case. Unless you're thinking about an insanity defense? I suppose I could go along with that, scream out hysterically in the middle of the night, strip naked and sit gibbering in the corner of my cell. I can't say I'd enjoy it but I'd go along with it if you think that's the answer. But—"

"Don't be ridiculous," Ehrengraf said, wrinkling his nose with distaste. "I mean to get you acquitted, Mr. Gort. Not committed to an asylum."

"I don't understand," Gort said. He frowned, looked around craftily. "You think the place is bugged," he whispered. "That's it, eh?"

"You can use your normal tone of voice. No, they don't employ hidden microphones in this jail. It's not only illegal but against policy as well."

"Then I don't understand. Look, I'm the guy who fastened the dynamite under the hood of Ginnie's Pontiac. I hooked up a cable to the starter. I set things up so that she would be blown into the next world. Now how do you propose to—"

"Mr. Gort." Ehrengraf held up a hand like a stop sign. "Please, Mr. Gort."

Alvin Gort subsided.

"Mr. Gort," Ehrengraf continued, "I defend the innocent and leave it to more clever men than myself to employ trickery in the cause of the guilty. And I find this very easy to do because all my clients are innocent. There is, you know, a legal principle involved."

"A legal principle?"

"The presumption of innocence."

"The presumption of—? Oh, you mean a man is presumed innocent until proven guilty."

"A tenet of Anglo-Saxon jurisprudence," Ehrengraf said. "The French presume guilt until innocence is proven. And the totalitarian countries, of course, presume guilt and do not allow innocence to be proved, taking it for granted that their police would not dream of wasting their time arresting the innocent in the first place. But I refer, Mr. Gort, to something more far-reaching than the legal presumption of innocence." Ehrengraf drew himself up to his full height, such as it was, and his back went ramrod straight. "I refer," he said, "to the Ehrengraf Presumption."

"The Ehrengraf Presumption?"

"Any client of Martin H. Ehrengraf," said Martin Ehrengraf, "is presumed by Ehrengraf to be innocent, which presumption is invariably confirmed in due course, the preconceptions of the client himself notwithstanding." The little lawyer smiled with his lips. "Now," he said, "shall we get down to business?"

Half an hour later Alvin Gort was still sitting on the edge of his cot. Martin Ehrengraf, however, was pacing briskly in the manner of a caged lion. With the thumb and forefinger of his right hand he smoothed the ends of his neat mustache. His left hand was at his side, its thumb hooked into his trouser pocket. He continued to pace while Gort smoked a cigarette almost to the filter. Then, as Gort ground the butt under his heel, Ehrengraf turned on his own heel and fixed his eyes on his client.

"The evidence is damning," he conceded. "A man of your description purchased dynamite and blasting caps from Tattersall Demolition Supply just ten days before your wife's death. Your signature is on the purchase order. A clerk remembers waiting on you and reports that you were nervous."

"Damn right I was nervous," Gort said. "I never killed anyone before."

"Please, Mr. Gort. If you must maintain the facade of having committed murder, at least keep your illusion to yourself. Don't share it with me. At the moment I'm concerned with evidence. We have your signature on the purchase order and we have you identified by the clerk. The man even remembers what you were wearing. Most customers come to Tattersall in work clothes, it would seem, while you wore a rather distinctive burgundy blazer and white flannel slacks. And tasseled loafers," he added, clearly not approving of them.

"It's hard to find casual loafers without tassels or braid these days."

"Hard, yes. But scarcely impossible. Now you say your wife had a lover, a Mr. Barry Lattimore."

"That toad Lattimore!"

"You knew of this affair and disapproved."

"Disapproved! I hated them. I wanted to strangle both of them. I wanted—"

"Please, Mr. Gort."

"I'm sorry."

Ehrengraf sighed. "Now your wife seems to have written a letter to her sister in New Mexico. She did in fact have a sister in New Mexico?"

"Her sister Grace. In Socorro."

"She posted the letter four days before her death. In it she stated that you knew about her affair with Lattimore."

"I'd known for weeks."

"She went on to say that she feared for her life. 'The situation is deteriorating and I don't know what to do. You know what a temper he has. I'm afraid he might be capable of anything, anything at all. I'm defenseless and I don't know what to do.'"

"Defenseless as a cobra," Gort muttered.

"No doubt. That was from memory but it's a fair approximation. Of course I'll have to examine the original. And I'll want specimens of your wife's handwriting."

"You can't think the letter's a forgery?"

"We never know, do we? But I'm sure you can tell me where I can get hold of samples. Now what other evidence do we have to contend with? There was a neighbor who saw you doing something under the hood of your wife's car some four or five hours before her death."

"Mrs. Boerland. Damned old crone. Vicious gossiping busybody."

"You seem to have been in the garage shortly before dawn. You had a light on and the garage door was open, and you had the hood of the car up and were doing something."

"Damned right I was doing something. I was—"

"Please, Mr. Gort. Between tasseled loafers and these constant interjections—"

"Won't happen again, Mr. Ehrengraf."

"Yes. Now just let me see. There were two cars in the garage, were there not? Your Buick and your wife's Pontiac. Your car was parked on the left-hand side, your wife's on the right."

"That was so that she could back straight out. When you're parked on the left side you have to back out in a sort of squiggly way. When Ginnie tried to do that she always ran over a corner of the lawn."

"Ah."

"Some people just don't give a damn about a lawn," Gort said, "and some people do."

"As with so many aspects of human endeavor, Mr. Gort. Now Mrs. Boerland observed you in the garage shortly before dawn, and the actual explosion which claimed your wife's life took place a few hours later while you were having your breakfast."

"Toasted English muffin and coffee. Years ago Ginnie made scrambled eggs and squeezed fresh orange juice for me. But with the passage of time—"

"Did she normally start her car at that hour?"

"No," Gort said. He sat up straight, frowned. "No, of course not. Dammit, why didn't I think of that? I figured she'd sit around the house until noon. I wanted to be well away from the place when it happened—"

"Mr. Gort."

"Well, I did. All of a sudden there was this shock wave and a thunderclap right on top of it and I'll tell you, Mr. Ehrengraf, I didn't even know what it was."

"Of course you didn't."

"I mean—"

"I wonder why your wife left the house at that hour. She said nothing to you?"

"No. There was a phone call and—"

"From whom?"

Gort frowned again. "Damned if I know. But she got the call just before she left. I wonder if there's a connection."

"I shouldn't doubt it. Who was your wife's heir, Mr. Gort? Who would inherit her money?"

"Money?" Gort grinned. "Ginnie didn't have a dime. I was her legal heir just as she was mine, but I was the one who had the money. All she left was the jewelry and clothing that my money paid for."

"Any insurance?"

"Exactly enough to pay your fee," Gort said, and grinned this time rather like a shark. "Except that I won't see a penny of it. Fifty thousand dollars, double indemnity for accidental death, and I think the insurance companies call murder an accident, although it's always struck me as rather purposeful. That makes one hundred thousand dollars, your fee to the penny, but none of it'll come my way."

"It's true that one cannot profit financially from a crime," Ehrengraf said. "But if you're found innocent—"

Gort shook his head. "Doesn't make any difference," he said. "I just learned this the other day. About the same time I was buying the dynamite, she was changing her beneficiary. The change went through in plenty of time. The whole hundred thousand goes to that rotter Lattimore."

"Now that," said Martin Ehrengraf, "is very interesting."

Two weeks and three days later Alvin Gort sat in a surprisingly comfortable straight-backed chair in Martin Ehrengraf's exceptionally cluttered office. He balanced a checkbook on his knee and carefully made out a check. The fountain pen he used had cost him $65. The lawyer's services, for which the check he was writing represented payment in full, had cost him considerably more, yet Gort, a good judge of value, thought Ehrengraf's fee a bargain and the pen overpriced.

"One hundred thousand dollars," he said, waving the check in the air to dry its ink. "I've put today's date on it but ask you to hold it until Monday morning before depositing it. I've instructed my broker to sell securities and transfer funds to my checking account. I don't normally maintain a balance sufficient to cover a check of this size."

"That's understandable."

"I'm glad something is. Because I'm damned if I can understand how you got me off the hook."

Ehrengraf allowed himself a smile. "My greatest obstacle was your own mental attitude," he said. "You honestly believed yourself to be guilty of your wife's death, didn't you?"

"But—"

"Ah, my dear Mr. Gort. You see, I *knew* you were innocent. The Ehrengraf Presumption assured me of that. I merely had to look for someone with the right sort of motive, and who should emerge but Mr. Barry Lattimore, your wife's lover and beneficiary, a man with a need for money and a man whose affair with your wife was reaching crisis proportions.

"It was clear to me that you were not the sort of man to commit murder in such an obvious fashion. Buying the dynamite openly, signing the purchase order with your own name—my dear Mr. Gort, you would never behave so foolishly! No, you had to have been framed, and clearly Lattimore was the man who had reason to frame you."

"And then they found things," Gort said.

"Indeed they did, once I was able to tell them where to look. Extraordinary what turned up! You would think Lattimore would have had the sense to get rid of all that, wouldn't you? But no, a burgundy blazer and a pair of white slacks, a costume identical to your own but tailored to Mr. Lattimore's frame, hung in the very back of his clothes closet. And in a drawer of his desk the police found half a dozen sheets of paper on which he'd practiced your signature until he was able to do quite a creditable job of writing it. By dressing like you and signing your name to the purchase order, he quite neatly put your neck in the noose."

"Incredible."

"He even copied your tasseled loafers. The police found a pair in his closet, and of course the man never habitually wore loafers of any sort. Of course he denied ever having seen the shoes before. Or the jacket, or the slacks, and of course he denied having practiced your signature."

Gort's eyes went involuntarily to Ehrengraf's own shoes. This time the lawyer was wearing black wing tips. His suit was dove gray and somewhat more sedately tailored than the brown one Gort had seen previously. His tie was maroon, his cuff links simple gold hexagons. The precision of Ehrengraf's dress and carriage contrasted sharply with the disarray of his office.

"And that letter from your wife to her sister Grace," Ehrengraf continued. "It turned out to be authentic, as it happens, but it also proved to be open to a second interpretation. The man of whom Virginia was afraid was never named, and a thoughtful reading showed he could as easily have been Lattimore as you. And then of course a second letter to Grace was found among your wife's effects. She evidently wrote it the night before her death and never had a chance to mail it. It's positively damning. She tells her sister how she changed the beneficiary of her insurance at Lattimore's insistence, how your knowledge of the affair was making Lattimore irrational and dangerous, and how she couldn't avoid the feeling that he planned to kill her. She goes on to say that she intended to change her insurance again, making Grace the beneficiary, and that she would so inform Lattimore in order to remove any financial motive for her murder.

"But even as she was writing those lines, he was preparing to put the dynamite in her car."

Ehrengraf went on explaining and Gort could only stare at him in wonder. Was it that his own memory could have departed so utterly from reality? Had the twin shocks of Ginnie's death and of his own arrest have caused him to fabricate a whole set of false memories?

Damn it, he *remembered* buying that dynamite! He *remembered* wiring it under the hood of her Pontiac! So how on earth—

The Ehrengraf Presumption, he thought. If Ehrengraf could presume Gort's innocence the way he did, why couldn't Gort presume his *own* innocence? Why not give himself the benefit of the doubt?

Because the alternative was terrifying. The letter, the practice sheets of his signature, the shoes and slacks and burgundy blazer—

"Mr. Gort? Are you all right?"

"I'm fine," Gort said.

"You looked pale for a moment. The strain, no doubt. Will you take a glass of water?"

"No, I don't think so." Gort lit a cigarette, inhaled deeply. "I'm fine," he said. "I feel good about everything. You know, not only am I in the clear but ultimately I don't think your fee will cost me anything."

"Oh?"

"Not if that rotter really and truly killed her. Lattimore can't profit from a murder he committed. And while she may have intended to make Grace her beneficiary, her unfulfilled intent has no legal weight. So her estate becomes the beneficiary of the insurance policy, and she never did get around to changing her will, so that means the money will wind up in my hands. Amazing, isn't it?"

"Amazing." The little lawyer rubbed his hands together briskly. "But you do know what they say about unhatched chickens, Mr. Gort. Mr. Lattimore hasn't been convicted of anything yet."

"You think he's got a chance of getting off?"

"That would depend," said Martin Ehrengraf, "on his choice of attorney."

≡

This time Ehrengraf's suit was navy blue with a barely perceptible stripe in a lighter blue. His shirt, as usual, was white. His shoes were black loafers—no tassels or braid—and his tie had a half-inch stripe of royal blue flanked by two narrower stripes, one of gold and the other of a rather bright green, all on a navy field. The necktie was that of the Caedmon Society of Oxford University, an organization of which Mr. Ehrengraf was not a member. The tie was a souvenir of another case and the lawyer wore it now and then on especially auspicious occasions.

Such as this visit to the cell of Barry Pierce Lattimore.

"I'm innocent," Lattimore said. "But it's gotten to the point where I don't expect anyone to believe me. There's so much evidence against me."

"Circumstantial evidence."

"Yes, but that's often enough to hang a man, isn't it?" Lattimore winced at the thought. "I loved Ginnie. I wanted to marry her. I never even thought of killing her."

"I believe you."

"You do?"

Ehrengraf nodded solemnly. "Indeed I do," he said. "Otherwise I wouldn't be here. I only collect fees when I get results, Mr. Lattimore. If I can't get you acquitted of all charges, then I won't take a penny for my trouble."

"That's unusual, isn't it?"

"It is."

"My own lawyer thinks I'm crazy to hire you. He had several criminal lawyers he was prepared to recommend. But I know a little about you. I know you get results. And since I *am* innocent, I feel I want to be represented by someone with a vested interest in getting me free."

"Of course my fees are high, Mr. Lattimore."

"Well, there's a problem. I'm not a rich man."

"You're the beneficiary of a hundred-thousand-dollar insurance policy."

"But I can't collect that money."

"You can if you're found innocent."

"Oh," Lattimore said. "Oh."

"And otherwise you'll owe me nothing."

"Then I can't lose, can I?"

"So it would seem," Ehrengraf said. "Now shall we begin? It's quite clear you were framed, Mr. Lattimore. That blazer and those trousers did not find their way to your closet of their own accord. Those shoes did not walk in by themselves. The two letters to Mrs. Gort's sister, one mailed and one unmailed, must have part of the scheme. Someone constructed an elaborate frame-up, Mr. Lattimore, with the object of implicating first Mr. Gort and then yourself. Now let's determine who would have a motive."

"Gort," said Lattimore.

"I think not."

"Who else? He had a reason to kill her. And he hated me, so who would have more reason to—"

"Mr. Lattimore, I'm afraid that's not a possibility. You see, Mr. Gort was a client of mine."

"Oh. Yes, I forgot."

"And I'm personally convinced of his innocence."

"I see."

"Just as I'm convinced of yours."

"I see."

"Now who else would have a motive? Was Mrs. Gort emotionally involved with anyone else? Did she have another lover? Had she had any other lovers before you came into the picture? And how about Mr. Gort? A former mistress who might have had a grudge against both him and his wife? Hmmm?" Ehrengraf smoothed the ends of his mustache. "Or perhaps, just perhaps, there was an elaborate plot hatched by *Mrs.* Gort."

"Ginnie?"

"It's not impossible. I'm afraid I must reject the possibility of suicide. It's tempting but in this instance I fear it just won't wash. But let's suppose, let's merely suppose, that Mrs. Gort decided to murder her husband and implicate you."

"Why would she do that?"

"I've no idea. But suppose she did, and suppose she intended to get her husband to drive her car and arranged the dynamite accordingly, and then when she left the house so hurriedly she forgot what she'd done, and of course the moment she turned the key in the ignition it all came back to her in a rather dramatic way."

"But I can't believe—"

"Oh, Mr. Lattimore," Ehrengraf said gently, "we believe what it pleases us to believe, don't you agree? The important thing is to recognize that you are innocent and to act on that recognition."

"But how can you be absolutely certain of my innocence?"

Martin Ehrengraf permitted himself a smile. "Mr. Lattimore," he said, "let me tell you about a principle of mine. I call it the Ehrengraf Presumption."

The EHRENGRAF Experience

"He who doubts from what he sees
Will ne'er believe, do what you please.
If the Sun and Moon should doubt,
They'd immediately go out."

—William Blake

Innocence," said Martin Ehrengraf. "There's the problem in a nutshell."

"Innocence is a problem?"

The little lawyer glanced around the prison cell, then turned to regard his client. "Precisely," he said. "If you weren't innocent you wouldn't be here."

"Oh, really?" Grantham Beale smiled, and while it was worthy of inclusion in a toothpaste commercial, it was the first smile he'd managed since his conviction on first-degree murder charges just two weeks and four days earlier. "Then you're saying that innocent men go to prison while guilty men walk free. Is that what you're saying?"

"It happens that way more than you might care to believe," Ehrengraf said softly. "But no, it is not what I am saying."

"Oh?"

"I am not contrasting innocence and guilt, Mr. Beale. I know you are innocent of murder. That is almost beside the point. All clients of Martin Ehrengraf are innocent of the crimes with which they are charged, and this innocence always emerges in due course. Indeed, this is more than a presumption on my part. It is the manner in which I make my living.

I set high fees, Mr. Beale, but I collect them only when my innocent clients emerge with their innocence a matter of public record. If my client goes to prison I collect nothing whatsoever, not even whatever expenses I incur on his behalf. So my clients are always innocent, Mr. Beale, just as you are innocent, in the sense that they are not guilty."

"Then why is my innocence a problem?"

"Ah, *your* innocence." Martin Ehrengraf smoothed the ends of his neatly trimmed mustache. His thin lips drew back in a smile, but the smile did not reach his deeply set dark eyes. He was, Grantham Beale noted, a superbly well-dressed little man, almost a dandy. He wore a Dartmouth green blazer with pearl buttons over a cream shirt with a tab collar. His slacks were flannel, modishly cuffed and pleated and the identical color of the shirt. His silk tie was a darker green than his jacket and sported a design in silver and bronze thread below the knot, a lion battling a unicorn. His cuff links matched his pearl blazer buttons. On his aristocratically small feet he wore highly polished seamless cordovan loafers, unadorned with tassels or braid, quite simple and quite elegant. Almost a dandy, Beale thought, but from what he'd heard the man had the skills to carry it off. He wasn't all front. He was said to get results.

"*Your* innocence," Ehrengraf said again. "Your innocence is not merely the innocence that is the opposite of guilt. It is the innocence that is the opposite of experience. Do you know Blake, Mr. Beale?"

"Blake?"

"William Blake, the poet. You wouldn't know him personally, of course. He's been dead for over a century. He wrote two books of poems early in his career, *Songs of Innocence* and *Songs of Experience*. Each poem in the one book had a counterpart in the other.

"Tyger, tyger, burning bright,
In the forests of the night,
What immortal hand or eye,
Could frame thy fearful symmetry?

"Perhaps that poem is familiar to you, Mr. Beale."

"I think I studied it in school."

"It's not unlikely. Well, you don't need a poetry lesson from me, sir, not in these depressing surroundings. Let me move a little more directly to the point. Innocence versus experience, Mr. Beale. You found yourself accused of a murder, sir, and you knew only that you had not committed it. And, being innocent not only of the murder itself but in Blake's sense of the word, you simply engaged a competent attorney and assumed matters would work themselves out in short order. We live in an enlightened democracy, Mr. Beale, and we grow up knowing that courts exist to free the innocent and the guilty, that no one gets away with murder."

"And that's all nonsense, eh?" Grantham Beale smiled his second smile since hearing the jury's verdict. If nothing else, he thought, the spiffy little lawyer improved a man's spirits.

"I wouldn't call it nonsense," Ehrengraf said. "But after all is said and done, you're in prison and the real murderer is not."

"Walker Murchison."

"I beg your pardon?"

"The real murderer," Grantham Beale said. "I'm in prison and Walker Gladstone Murchison is free."

"Precisely. Because it is not enough to be guiltless, Mr. Beale. One must also be able to convince a jury of one's guiltlessness. In short, had you been less innocent and more experienced, you could have taken steps early on to assure you would not find yourself in your present condition right now."

"And what could I have done?"

"What you *have* done, at long last," said Martin Ehrengraf. "You could have called me immediately."

═══

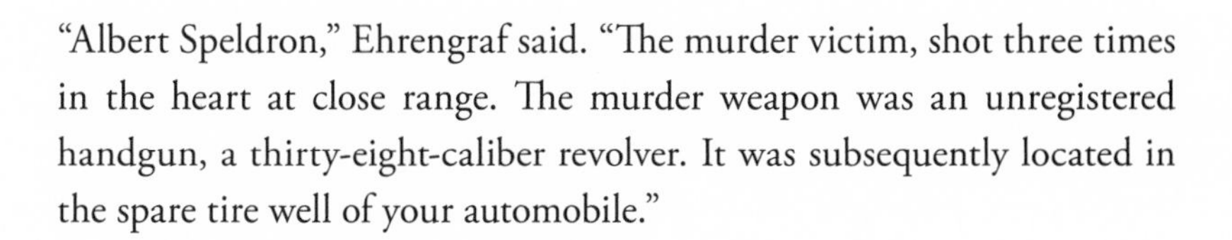

"Albert Speldron," Ehrengraf said. "The murder victim, shot three times in the heart at close range. The murder weapon was an unregistered handgun, a thirty-eight-caliber revolver. It was subsequently located in the spare tire well of your automobile."

"It wasn't my gun. I never saw it in my life until the police showed it to me."

"Of course you didn't," Ehrengraf said soothingly. "To continue. Albert Speldron was a loan shark. Not, however, the sort of gruff-voiced thug who lends ten or twenty dollars at a time to longshoremen and factory hands and breaks their legs with a baseball bat if they're late paying the vig."

"Paying the what?"

"Ah, sweet innocence," Ehrengraf said. "The vig. Short for vigorish. It's a term used by the criminal element to describe the ongoing interest payments which a debtor must make to maintain his status."

"I never heard the term," Beale said, "but I paid it well enough. I paid Speldron a thousand dollars a week and that didn't touch the principal."

"And you had borrowed how much?"

"Fifty thousand dollars."

"The jury apparently considered that a satisfactory motive for murder."

"Well, that's crazy," said. "Why on earth would I want to kill Speldron? I didn't hate the man. He'd done me a service by lending me that money. I had a chance to buy a valuable stamp collection. That's my business, I buy and sell stamps, and I had an opportunity to get hold of an extraordinary collection, mostly U.S. and British Empire but a really exceptional lot of early German States as well, and there were also—well, before I get carried away, are you interested in stamps at all?"

"Only when I've a letter to mail."

"Oh. Well, this was a fine collection, let me say that much and leave it at that. The seller had to have all cash and the transaction had to go unrecorded. Taxes, you understand."

"Indeed I do. The system of taxation makes criminals of us all."

"I don't really think of it as criminal," Beale said.

"Few people do. But go on, sir."

"What more is there to say? I had to raise fifty thousand dollars on the quiet to close the deal on this fine lot of stamps. By dealing with Speldron, I was able to borrow the money without filling out a lot of forms or giving him anything but my word. I was quite confident I would triple my money by the time I broke up the collection and sold it in job lots to a variety of dealers and collectors. I'll probably take in a total of fifty thousand out of the U.S. issues alone, and I know a buyer who will salivate when he gets a look at the German States issues."

"So it didn't bother you to pay Speldron his thousand a week."

"Not a bit. I figured to have half the stamps sold within a couple of months, and the first thing I'd do would be to repay the fifty thousand dollars principal and close out the loan. I'd have paid eight or ten thousand dollars in interest, say, but what's that compared to a profit of fifty or a hundred thousand dollars? Speldron was doing me a favor and I appreciated it. Oh, he was doing himself a favor too, two percent interest per week didn't put him in the hardship category, but it was just good business for both of us, no question about it."

"You'd dealt with him before?"

"Maybe a dozen times over the years. I've borrowed sums ranging between ten and seventy thousand dollars. I never heard the interest payments called vigorish before, but I always paid them promptly. And no one ever threatened to break my legs. We did business together, Speldron and I. And it always worked out very well for both of us."

"The prosecution argued that by killing Speldron you erased your debt to him. That's certainly a motive a jury can understand, Mr. Beale. In a world where men are commonly killed for the price of a bottle of whiskey, fifty thousand dollars does seem enough to kill a man over."

"But I'd be crazy to kill for that sum. I'm not a pauper. If I was having trouble paying Speldron all I had to do was sell the stamps."

"And if you had trouble selling them?"

"Then I could have liquidated other merchandise from my stock. I could have mortgaged my home. Why, I could have raised enough on the house to pay off Speldron three times over. That car they found the gun in, that's an Antonelli Scorpion. The car alone is worth more than I owed Speldron."

"Indeed," Martin Ehrengraf said. "But this Walker Murchison. How does he come into the picture?"

"He killed Speldron."

"How do we know this, Mr. Beale?"

Grantham Beale got to his feet. He'd been sitting on his iron cot, leaving the cell's one chair for the lawyer. Now he stood up, stretched, and walked to the rear of the cell. For a moment he stood regarding some graffito on the cell wall. Then he turned and looked at Ehrengraf.

"Speldron and Murchison were partners," he said. "I dealt only with Speldron because Murchison steered clear of unsecured loans. And Murchison had an insurance business in which Speldron did not participate. Their joint ventures included real estate, investments, and other activities where large sums of money moved around quickly with few records kept of exactly what took place."

"Shady operations," Ehrengraf said.

"For the most part. Not always illegal, not entirely illegal, but, yes, I like your word. Shady."

"So they were partners, and it is not unheard of for one to kill one's partner. To dissolve a partnership by the most direct means available, as it were. But why this partnership? Why should Murchison kill Speldron?"

Beale shrugged. "Money," he suggested. "With all that cash floating around, you can bet Murchison made out handsomely on Speldron's death. I'll bet he put a lot more than fifty thousand unrecorded dollars into his pocket."

"That's your only reason for suspecting him?"

Beale shook his head. "The partnership had a secretary," he said. "Her name's Felicia. Young, long dark hair, flashing dark eyes, a body like a magazine centerfold, and a face like a Chanel ad. Both of the partners were sleeping with her."

"Perhaps this was not a source of enmity."

"But it was. Murchison's married to her."

"Ah."

"But there's an important reason why I know it was Murchison who killed Speldron." Beale stepped forward, stood over the seated attorney. "The gun was found in the boot of my car," he said. "Wrapped in a filthy towel and stuffed in the spare tire well. There were no fingerprints on the gun and it wasn't registered to me but there it was in my car."

"The Antonelli Scorpion?"

"Yes. What of it?"

"No matter."

Beale frowned momentarily, then drew a breath and plunged onward. "It was put there to frame me," he said.

"So it would seem."

"It had to be put there by somebody who knew I owed Speldron money. Somebody with inside information. The two of them were partners. I met Murchison any number of times when I went to the office to pay the interest, or vigorish as you called it. Why do they call it that?"

"I've no idea."

"Murchison knew I owed money. And Murchison and I never liked each other."

"Why?"

"We just didn't get along. The reason's not important. And there's more, I'm not just grasping at straws. It was Murchison who suggested I might have killed Speldron. A lot of men owed Speldron money and there were probably several of them who were in much stickier shape financially than I, but Murchison told the police I'd had a loud and bitter argument with Speldron two days before he was killed!"

"And had you?"

"No! Why, I never in my life argued with Speldron."

"Interesting." The little lawyer raised his hand to his mustache, smoothing its tips delicately. His nails were manicured, Grantham Beale noted, and was there colorless nail polish on them? No, he observed, there was not. The little man might be something of a dandy but he was evidently not a fop.

"Did you indeed meet with Mr. Speldron on the day in question?"

"Yes, as a matter of fact I did. I made the interest payment and we exchanged pleasantries. There was nothing anyone could have mistaken for an argument."

"Ah."

"And even if there had been, Murchison wouldn't have known about it. He wasn't even in the office."

"Still more interesting," Ehrengraf said thoughtfully.

"It certainly is. But how can you possibly prove that he murdered his partner and framed me for it? You can't trap him into confessing, can you?"

"Murderers do confess."

"Not Murchison. You could try tracing the gun to him, I suppose, but the police tried to link it to me and found they couldn't trace it at all. I just don't see—"

"Mr. Beale."

"Yes?"

"Why don't you sit down, Mr. Beale. Here, take this chair, I'm sure it's more comfortable than the edge of the bed. I'll stand for a moment. Mr. Beale, do you have a dollar?"

"They don't let us have money here."

"Then take this. It's a dollar which I'm lending to you." The lawyer's dark eyes glinted. "No interest, Mr. Beale. A personal loan, not a business transaction. Now, sir, please give me the dollar which I've just lent to you."

"Give it to you?"

"That's right. Thank you. You have retained me, Mr. Beale, to look after your interests. The day you are released from this prison you will owe me a fee of ninety thousand dollars. The fee will be all inclusive. Any expenses will be mine to bear. Should I fail to secure your release you will owe me nothing."

"But—"

"Is that agreeable, sir?"

"But what are you going to do? Engage detectives? File an appeal? Try to get the case reopened?"

"When a man engages to save your life, Mr. Beale, do you require that he first outline his plans for you?"

"No, but—"

"Ninety thousand dollars. Payable if I succeed. Are the terms agreeable?"

"Yes, but—"

"Mr. Beale, when next we meet you will owe me ninety thousand dollars plus whatever emotional gratitude comes naturally to you. Until then, sir, you owe me one dollar." The thin lips curled in a shadowy smile. "'The cut worm forgives the plow,' Mr. Beale. William Blake, *The Marriage of Heaven and Hell.* 'The cut worm forgives the plow.' You might think about that, sir, until we meet again."

The second meeting of Martin Ehrengraf and Grantham Beale took place five weeks and four days later. On this occasion the little lawyer wore a navy two-button suit with a subtle vertical stripe. His shoes were highly polished black wing tips, his shirt a pale blue broadcloth with contrasting white collar and cuffs. His necktie bore a half-inch wide stripe of royal blue flanked by two narrower strips, one gold and the other a rather bright green, all on a navy field.

And this time Ehrengraf's client was also rather nicely turned out, although his tweed jacket and flannels were hardly a match for the lawyer's suit. But Beale's dress was a great improvement over the shapeless gray prison garb he had worn previously, just as his office, a room filled with jumbled books and boxes, a desk covered with books and albums and stamps in and out of glassine envelopes, two worn leather chairs, and a matching sagging sofa—just as all of this comfortable disarray was a vast improvement over the prison cell which had been the site of their earlier meeting.

Beale, seated behind his desk, gazed thoughtfully at Ehrengraf, who stood ramrod straight, one hand on the desk top, the other at his side. "Ninety thousand dollars," Beale said levelly. "You must admit that's a bit rich, Mr. Ehrengraf."

"We agreed on the price."

"No argument. We did agree, and I'm a firm believer in the sanctity of verbal agreements. But it was my understanding that your fee would be payable if my liberty came about as a result of your efforts."

"You are free today."

"I am indeed, and I'll be free tomorrow, but I can't see how it was any of your doing."

"Ah," Ehrengraf said. His face bore an expression of infinite disappointment, a disappointment felt not so much with this particular client as with the entire human race. "You feel I did nothing for you."

"I wouldn't say that. Perhaps you were taking steps to file an appeal. Perhaps you engaged detectives or did some detective work of your own. Perhaps in due course you would have found a way to get me out of prison, but in the meantime the unexpected happened and your services turned out to be unnecessary."

"The unexpected happened?"

"Well, who could have possibly anticipated it?" Beale shook his head in wonder. "Just think of it. Murchison went and got an attack of conscience. The bounder didn't have enough of a conscience to step forward and admit what he'd done, but he got to wondering what would happen if he died suddenly and I had to go on serving a life sentence for a crime he had committed. He wouldn't do anything to jeopardize his liberty while he lived but he wanted to be able to make amends if and when he died."

"Yes."

"So he prepared a letter," Beale went on. "Typed out a long letter explaining just why he had wanted his partner dead and how the unregistered gun had actually belonged to Speldron in the first place, and how he'd shot him and wrapped the gun in a towel and planted it in my car. Then he'd made up a story about my having had a fight with Albert Speldron, and of course that got the police looking in my direction, and the next thing I knew I was in jail. I saw the letter Murchison wrote. The police let me look at it. He went into complete detail."

"Considerate of him."

"And then he did the usual thing. Gave the letter to a lawyer with instructions that it be kept in his safe and opened only in the event of his death." Beale found a pair of stamp tongs in the clutter atop his desk, used them to lift a stamp, frowned at it for a moment, then set it down and looked directly at Martin Ehrengraf. "Do you suppose he had a premonition? For God's sake, Murchison was a young man, his health was good, and why should he anticipate dying? Maybe he did have a premonition."

"I doubt it."

"Then it's certainly a remarkable coincidence. A matter of weeks after turning this letter over to a lawyer, Murchison lost control of his car on a curve. Smashed right through the guard rail, plunged a couple of hundred feet, exploded on impact. I don't suppose the man knew what had happened to him."

"I suspect you're right."

"He was always a safe driver," Beale mused. "Perhaps he'd been drinking."

"Perhaps."

"And if he hadn't been decent enough to write that letter, I might be spending the rest of my life behind bars."

"How fortunate for you things turned out as they did."

"Exactly," Beale said. "And so, although I truly appreciate what you've done on my behalf, whatever that may be, and although I don't doubt you could have secured my liberty in due course, although I'm sure I don't know how you might have managed it, nevertheless as far as your fee is concerned—"

"Mr. Beale."

"Yes?"

"Do you really believe that a detestable troll like W. G. Murchison would take pains to arrange for your liberty in the event of his death?"

"Well, perhaps I misjudged the man. Perhaps—"

"Murchison hated you, Mr. Beale. If he found he was dying his one source of satisfaction would have been the knowledge that you were in prison for a crime you hadn't committed. I told you that you were an innocent, Mr. Beale, and a few weeks in prison has not dented or dulled your innocence. You actually think Murchison wrote that note."

'You mean he didn't?"

"It was typed upon a machine in his office," the lawyer said. "His own stationery was used, and the signature at the bottom is one many an expert would swear is Murchison's own."

"But he didn't write it?"

"Of course not." Martin Ehrengraf's hands hovered in the air before him. They might have been poised over an invisible typewriter or they might merely be looming as the talons of a bird of prey.

Grantham Beale stared at the little lawyer's hands in fascination. "You typed that letter," he said.

Ehrengraf shrugged.

"You—but Murchison left it with a lawyer!"

"The lawyer was not one Murchison had used in the past. Murchison evidently selected a stranger from the Yellow Pages, as far as one can determine, and made contact with him over the telephone, explaining what he wanted the man to do for him. He then mailed the letter along with a postal money order to cover the attorney's fee and a covering note confirming the telephone conversation. It seems he did not use his own name in his discussions with his lawyer, and he signed an alias to his covering note and to the money order as well. The signature he wrote, though, does seem to be in his own handwriting."

Ehrengraf paused, and his right hand went to finger the knot of his necktie. This particular tie, rather more colorful than his usual choice, was that of the Caedmon Society of Oxford University, an organization to which Martin Ehrengraf did not belong. The tie was a souvenir of an earlier case and he tended to wear it on particularly happy occasions, moments of personal triumph.

"Murchison left careful instructions," he went on. "He would call the lawyer every Thursday, merely repeating the alias he had used. If ever a Thursday passed without a call, and if there was no call on Friday either, the lawyer was to open the letter and follow its instructions. For four Thursdays in a row the lawyer received a phone call, presumably from Murchison."

"Presumably," Beale said heavily.

"Indeed. On the Tuesday following the fourth Thursday, Murchison's car went off a cliff and he was killed instantly. The lawyer read of Walker Murchison's death but had no idea that was his client's true identity. Then Thursday came and went without a call, and when there was no telephone call Friday either, why, the dutiful attorney opened the letter and went forthwith to the police." Ehrengraf spread his hands, smiled broadly. "The rest," he said, "you know as well as I."

"Great Scott," Beale said.

"Now if you honestly feel I've done nothing to earn my money—"

"I'll have to liquidate some stock," Beale said. "It won't be a problem and there shouldn't be much time involved. I'll bring a check to your office in a week. Say ten days at the outside. Unless you'd prefer cash?"

"A check will be fine, Mr. Beale. So long as it's a good check." And he smiled with his lips to show he was joking.

The smile gave Beale a chill.

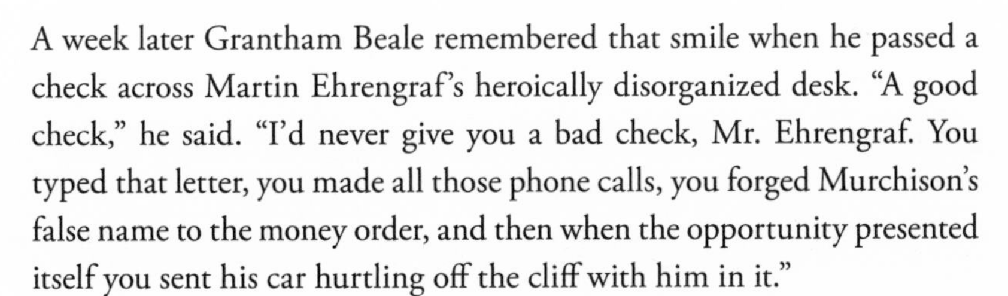

A week later Grantham Beale remembered that smile when he passed a check across Martin Ehrengraf's heroically disorganized desk. "A good check," he said. "I'd never give you a bad check, Mr. Ehrengraf. You typed that letter, you made all those phone calls, you forged Murchison's false name to the money order, and then when the opportunity presented itself you sent his car hurtling off the cliff with him in it."

"One believes what one wishes," Ehrengraf said quietly.

"I've been thinking about all of this all week long. Murchison framed me for a murder he committed, then paid for the crime himself and liberated me in the process without knowing what he was doing. 'The cut worm forgives the plow.'"

"Indeed."

"Meaning that the end justifies the means."

"Is that what Blake meant by that line? I've long wondered."

"The end justifies the means. I'm innocent, and now I'm free, and Murchison's guilty, and now he's dead, and you've got the money, but that's all right, because I made out fine on those stamps, and of course I don't have to repay Speldron, poor man, because death did cancel that particular debt, and—"

"Mr. Beale."

"Yes?"

"I don't know if I should tell you this, but I fear I must. You are more of an innocent than you realize. You've paid me handsomely for my services, as indeed we agreed that you would, and I think perhaps I'll offer you a lagniappe in the form of some experience to offset your colossal innocence. I'll begin with some advice. Do not, under any circumstances, resume your affair with Felicia Murchison."

Beale stared.

"You should have told me that was why you and Murchison didn't get along," Ehrengraf said gently. "I was forced to discover it for myself. No matter. More to the point, one should not share a pillow with a woman who has so little regard for one as to frame one for murder. Mrs. Murchison—"

"Felicia framed me?"

"Of course, Mr. Beale. Mrs. Murchison had nothing against you. It was sufficient that she had nothing for you. She murdered Mr. Speldron, you see, for reasons which need hardly concern us. Then having done so she needed someone to be cast as the murderer.

"Her husband could hardly have told the police about your purported argument with Speldron. He wasn't around at the time. He didn't know the two of you had met, and if he went out on a limb and told them, and then you had an alibi for the time in question, why, he'd wind up looking silly, wouldn't he? But Mrs. Murchison knew you'd met with Speldron, and she told her husband the two of you argued, and so he told the police in perfectly good faith what she had told him, and then they went and found the murder gun in your very own Antonelli Scorpion. A stunning automobile, incidentally, and it's to your credit to own such a vehicle, Mr. Beale."

"Felicia killed Speldron."

"Yes."

"And framed me."

"Yes."

"But—why did you frame Murchison?"

"Did you expect me to try to convince the powers that be that she did it? And had pangs of conscience and left a letter with a lawyer?

Women don't leave letters with lawyers, Mr. Beale, any more than they have consciences. One must deal with the materials at hand."

"But—"

"And the woman is young, with long dark hair, flashing dark eyes, a body like a magazine centerfold, and a face like a Chanel ad. She's also an excellent typist and most cooperative in any number of ways which we needn't discuss at the moment. Mr. Beale, would you like me to get you a glass of water?"

"I'm all right."

"I'm sure you'll be all right, Mr. Beale. I'm sure you will. Mr. Beale, I'm going to make a suggestion. I think you should seriously consider marrying and settling down. I think you'd be much happier that way. You're an innocent, Mr. Beale, and you've had the Ehrengraf Experience now, and it's rendered you considerably more experienced than you were, but your innocence is not the sort to be readily vanquished. Give the widow Murchison and all her tribe a wide berth, Mr. Beale. They're not for you. Find yourself an old-fashioned girl and lead a proper old-fashioned life. Buy and sell stamps. Cultivate a garden. Raise terriers. The West Highland White might be a good breed for you but that's your decision, certainly. Mr. Beale? Are you *sure* you won't have a glass of water?"

"I'm all right."

"Quite. I'll leave you with another thought of Blake's, Mr. Beale. 'Lilies that fester smell worse than weeds.' That's also from *The Marriage of Heaven and Hell*, another of what he calls Proverbs of Hell, and perhaps someday you'll be able to interpret it for me. I never quite know for sure what Blake's getting at, Mr. Beale, but his things do have a nice sound to them, don't they? Innocence and experience, Mr. Beale. That's the ticket, isn't it? Innocence and experience."

The EHRENGRAF Appointment

"Dame Fortune is a fickle gypsy,
And always blind, and often tipsy."
—William Mackworth Praed

Martin Ehrengraf was walking jauntily down the courthouse steps when a taller and bulkier man caught up with him. "Glorious day," the man said. "Simply a glorious day."

Ehrengraf nodded. It was indeed a glorious day, the sort of autumn afternoon that made men recall football weekends. Ehrengraf had just been thinking that he'd like a piece of hot apple pie with a slab of sharp cheddar on it. He rarely thought about apple pie and almost never wanted cheese on it, but it was that sort of day.

"I'm Cutliffe," the man said. "Hudson Cutliffe, of Marquardt, Stoner, and Cutliffe."

"Ehrengraf," said Ehrengraf.

"Yes, I know. Oh, believe me, I know." Cutliffe gave what he doubtless considered a hearty chuckle. "Imagine running into Martin Ehrengraf himself, standing in line for an IDC appointment just like everybody else."

"Every man is entitled to a proper defense," Ehrengraf said stiffly. "It's a guaranteed right in a free society."

"Yes, to be sure, but—"

"Indigent defendants have attorneys appointed by the court. Our system here calls for attorneys to make themselves available at specified intervals for such appointments, rather than entrust such cases to a public defender."

"I quite understand," Cutliffe said. "Why, I was just appointed to an IDC case myself, some luckless chap who stole a satchel full of meat from a supermarket. Choice cuts, too—lamb chops, filet mignon. You just about have to steal them these days, don't you?"

Ehrengraf, a recent convert to vegetarianism, offered a thin-lipped smile and thought about pie and cheese.

"But Martin Ehrengraf himself," Cutliffe went on. "One no more thinks of you in this context than one imagines a glamorous Hollywood actress going to the bathroom. Martin Ehrengraf, the dapper and debonair lawyer who hardly ever appears in court. The man who only collects a fee if he wins. Is that really true, by the way? You actually take murder cases on a contingency basis?"

"That's correct."

"Extraordinary. I don't see how you can possibly afford to operate that way."

"It's quite simple," Ehrengraf said.

"Oh?"

His smile was fuller than before. "I always win," he said. "It's simplicity itself."

"And yet you rarely appear in court."

"Sometimes one can work more effectively behind the scenes."

"And when your client wins his freedom—"

"I'm paid in full," Ehrengraf said.

"Your fees are high, I understand."

"Exceedingly high."

"And your clients almost always get off."

"They're always innocent," Ehrengraf said. "That does help."

Hudson Cutliffe laughed richly, as if to suggest that the idea of bringing guilt and innocence into a discussion of legal procedures was amusing. "Well, this will be a switch for you," he said at length. "You were assigned the Protter case, weren't you?"

"Mr. Protter is my client, yes."

"Hardly a typical Ehrengraf case, is it? Man gets drunk, beats his wife to death, passes out, and sleeps it off, then wakes up and sees what he's done and calls the police. Bit of luck for you, wouldn't you say?"

"Oh?"

"Won't take up too much of your time. You'll plead him guilty to manslaughter, get a reduced sentence on grounds of his previous clean record, and then Protter'll do a year or two in prison while you go about your business."

"You think that's the course to pursue, Mr. Cutliffe?"

"It's what anyone would do."

"Almost anyone," said Ehrengraf.

"And there's no reason to make work for yourself, is there?" Cutliffe winked. "These IDC cases—I don't know why they pay us at all, as small as the fees are. A hundred and seventy-five dollars isn't much of an all-inclusive fee for a legal defense, is it? Wouldn't you say your average fee runs a bit higher than that?"

"Quite a bit higher."

"But there are compensations. It's the same hundred and seventy-five dollars whether you plead your client or stand trial, let alone win. A far cry from your usual system, eh, Ehrengraf? You don't have to win to get paid."

"I do," Ehrengraf said.

"How's that?"

"If I lose the case, I'll donate the fee to charity."

"If you lose? But you'll plead him to manslaughter, won't you?"

"Certainly not."

"Then what will you do?"

"I'll plead him innocent."

"Innocent?"

"Of course. The man never killed anyone."

"But—" Cutliffe inclined his head, dropped his voice. "You know the man? You have some special information about the case?"

"I've never met him and know only what I've read in the newspapers."

"Then how can you say he's innocent?"

"He's my client."

"So?"

"I do not represent the guilty," Ehrengraf said. "My clients are innocent, Mr. Cutliffe, and Arnold Protter is a client of mine, and I intend to earn my fee as his attorney, however inadequate that fee may be. I did not seek appointment, Mr. Cutliffe, but that appointment is a sacred trust, sir, and I shall justify that trust. Good day, Mr. Cutliffe."

"They said they'd get me a lawyer and it wouldn't cost me nothing," Arnold Protter said. "I guess you're it, huh?"

"Indeed," said Ehrengraf. He glanced around the sordid little jail cell, then cast an eye on his new client. Arnold Protter was a thickset round-shouldered man in his late thirties with the ample belly of a beer drinker and the red nose of a whiskey drinker. His pudgy face recalled the Pillsbury Dough Boy. His hands, too, were pudgy, and he held them out in front of his red nose and studied them in wonder.

"These were the hands that did it," he said.

"Nonsense."

"How's that?"

"Perhaps you'd better tell me what happened," Ehrengraf suggested. "The night your wife was killed."

"It's hard to remember," Protter said.

"I'm sure it is."

"What it was, it was an ordinary kind of a night. Me and Gretch had a beer or two during the afternoon, just passing time while we watched television. Then we ordered up a pizza and had a couple more with it, and then we settled in for the evening and started hitting the boilermakers. You know, a shot and a beer. First thing you know, we're having this argument."

"About what?"

Protter got up, paced, glared again at his hands. He lumbered about, Ehrengraf thought, like a caged bear. His chino pants were ragged at the cuffs and his plaid shirt was a tartan no Highlander would recognize.

Ehrengraf, in contrast, sparkled in the drab cell like a diamond on a dust-heap. His suit was a herringbone tweed the color of a well-smoked briar pipe, and beneath it he wore a suede doeskin vest over a cream broadcloth shirt with French cuffs and a tab collar. His cufflinks were simple gold hexagons, his tie a wool knit in the same brown as his suit. His shoes were shell cordovan loafers, quite simple and elegant and polished to a high sheen.

"The argument," Ehrengraf prompted.

"Oh, I don't know how it got started," Protter said. "One thing led to another, and pretty soon she's making a federal case over me and this woman who lives one flight down from us."

"What woman?"

"Her name's Agnes Mullane. Gretchen's giving me the business that me and Agnes got something going."

"And were you having an affair with Agnes Mullane?"

"Naw, 'course not. Maybe me and Agnes'd pass the time of day on the staircase, and maybe I had some thoughts on the subject, but nothing ever came of it. But she started in on the subject, Gretch did, and to get a little of my own back I started ragging her about this guy lives one flight up from us."

"And his name is—"

"Gates, Harry Gates."

"You thought your wife was having an affair with Gates?"

Protter shook his head. "Naw, 'course not. But he's an artist, Gates is, and I was accusing her of posing for him, you know. Naked. No clothes on."

"Nude."

"Yeah."

"And did your wife pose for Mr. Gates?"

"You kidding? You never met Gretchen, did you?"

Ehrengraf shook his head.

"Well, Gretch was all right, and the both of us was used to each other, if you know what I mean, but you wouldn't figure her for somebody who woulda been Miss America if she coulda found her way to Atlantic City. And Gates, what would he need with a model?"

"You said he was an artist."

"He says he's an artist," Protter said, "but you couldn't prove it by me. What he paints don't look like nothing. I went up there one time on account of his radio's cooking at full blast, you know, and I want to ask him to put a lid on it, and he's up on top of this stepladder dribbling paint on a canvas that he's got spread out all over the floor. All different colors of paint, and he's just throwing them down at the canvas like a little kid making a mess."

"Then he's an abstract expressionist," Ehrengraf said.

"Naw, he's a painter. I mean, people buy these pictures of his. Not enough to make him rich or he wouldn't be living in the same dump with me and Gretch, but he makes a living at it. Enough to keep him in beer and pizza and all, but what would he need with a model? Only reason he'd want Gretchen up there is to hold the ladder steady."

"An abstract expressionist," said Ehrengraf. "That's very interesting. He lives directly above you, Mr. Protter?"

"Right upstairs, yeah. That's why we could hear his radio clear as a bell."

"Was it playing the night you and your wife drank the boilermakers?"

"We drank boilermakers lots of the time," Protter said, puzzled. "Oh, you mean the night I killed her."

"The night she died."

"Same thing, ain't it?"

"Not at all," said Ehrengraf. "But let it go. Was Mr. Gates playing his radio that night?"

Protter scratched his head. "Hard to remember," he said. "One night's like another, know what I mean? Yeah, the radio was going that night. I remember now. He was playing country music on it. Usually he plays that rock and roll, and that stuff gives me a headache, but this time it was country music. Country music, it sort of soothes my nerves." He frowned. "But I never played it on my own radio."

"Why was that?"

"Gretch hated it. Couldn't stand it, said the singers all sounded like dogs that ate poisoned meat and was dying of it. Gretch didn't like any music much. What she liked was the television, and then we'd have Gates with his rock and roll at top volume, and sometimes you'd hear a little country music coming upstairs from Agnes's radio. She liked country music, but she never played it very loud. With the windows open on a hot day you'd hear it, but otherwise no. Of course what you hear most with the windows open is the Puerto Ricans on the street with their transistor radios."

Protter went on at some length about Puerto Ricans and transistor radios. When he paused for breath, Ehrengraf straightened up and smiled with his lips. "A pleasure," he said. "Mr. Protter, I believe in your innocence."

"Huh?"

"You've been the victim of an elaborate and diabolical frame-up, sir. But you're in good hands now. Maintain your silence and put your faith in me. Is there anything you need to make your stay here more comfortable?"

"It's not so bad."

"Well, you won't be here for long. I'll see to that. Perhaps I can arrange for a radio for you. You could listen to country music."

"Be real nice," Protter said. "Soothing is what it is. It soothes my nerves."

An hour after his interview with his client, Ehrengraf was seated on a scarred wooden bench at a similarly distressed oaken table. The restaurant in which he was dining ran to college pennants and German beer steins suspended from the exposed dark wood beams. Ehrengraf was eating hot apple pie topped with sharp cheddar, and at the side of his plate was a small glass of neat Calvados.

The little lawyer was just preparing to take his first sip of the tangy apple brandy when a familiar voice sounded beside him.

"Ehrengraf," Hudson Cutliffe boomed out. "Fancy finding you here. Twice in one day, eh?"

Ehrengraf looked up, smiled. "Excellent pie here," he said.

"Come here all the time," Cutliffe said. "My home away from home. Never seen you here before, I don't think."

"My first time."

"Pie with cheese. If I ate that I'd put on ten pounds." Unbidden, the hefty attorney drew back the bench opposite Ehrengraf and seated himself. When a waiter appeared, Cutliffe ordered a slice of prime rib and a spinach salad.

"Watching my weight," he said. "Protein, that's the ticket. Got to cut down on the nasty old carbs. Well, Ehrengraf, I suppose you've seen your wife-murderer now, haven't you? Or are you still maintaining he's no murderer at all?"

"Protter's an innocent man."

Cutliffe chuckled. "Commendable attitude, I'm sure, but why don't you save it for the courtroom? The odd juryman may be impressed by that line of country. I'm not, myself. I've always found facts more convincing than attitudes."

"Indeed," said Ehrengraf. "Personally, I've always noticed the shadow as much as the substance. I suspect it's a difference of temperament, Mr. Cutliffe. I don't suppose you're much of a fan of poetry, are you?"

"Poetry? You mean rhymes and verses and all that?"

"More or less."

"Schoolboy stuff, eh? Boy stood on the burning deck, that the sort of thing you mean? Had a bellyful of that in school." He smiled suddenly. "Unless you're talking about limericks. I like the odd limerick now and then, I must say. Are you much of a hand for limericks?"

"Not really," said Ehrengraf.

Cutliffe delivered four limericks while Ehrengraf sat with a pained expression on his face. The first concerned a mathematician named Paul, the second a young harlot named Dinah, the third a man from Fort Ord, and the fourth an old woman from Truk.

"It's interesting," Ehrengraf said at length. "On the surface there's no similarity whatsoever between the limerick and abstract expressionist painting. They're not at all alike. And yet they are."

"I don't follow you."

"It's not important," Ehrengraf said. The waiter appeared, setting a plateful of rare beef in front of Cutliffe, who at once reached for his knife and fork. Ehrengraf looked at the meat. "You're going to eat that," he said.

"Of course. What else would I do with it?"

Ehrengraf took another small sip of the Calvados. Holding the glass aloft, he began an apparently aimless dissertation upon the innocence of his client. "If you were a reader of poetry," he found himself saying, "and if you did not systematically dull your sensibilities by consuming the flesh of beasts, Mr. Protter's innocence would be obvious to you."

"You're serious about defending him, then. You're really going to plead him innocent."

"How could I do otherwise?"

Cutliffe raised an eyebrow while lowering a fork. "You realize you're letting an idle whim jeopardize a man's liberty, Ehrengraf. Your Mr. Protter will surely receive a stiffer sentence after he's been found guilty by a jury, and—"

"But he won't be found guilty."

"Are you counting on some technicality to get him off the hook? Because I have a friend in the District Attorney's office, you know, and I went round there while you were visiting your client. He tells me the state's case is gilt-edged."

"The state is welcome to the gilt," Ehrengraf said grandly. "Mr. Protter has the innocence."

Cutliffe put down his fork, set his jaw. "Perhaps," he said, "perhaps you simply do not care. Perhaps, having no true financial stake in Arnold Protter's fate, you just don't give a damn what happens to him. Whereas, had you a substantial sum riding on the outcome of the case—"

"Oh, dear," said Ehrengraf. "You're not by any chance proposing a wager?"

≡

Miss Agnes Mullane had had a permanent recently, and her copper-colored hair looked as though she'd stuck her big toe in an electric socket. She had a freckled face, a pug nose, and a body that would send whole shifts of construction workers plummeting from their scaffolds. She wore a hostess outfit of a silky green fabric, and her walk, Ehrengraf noted, was decidedly slinky.

"So terrible about the Protters," she said. "They were good neighbors, although I never became terribly close with either of them. She kept to herself, for the most part, but he always had a smile and a cheerful word for me when I would run into him on the stairs. Of course I've always gotten on better with men than with women, Mr. Ehrengraf, though I'm sure I couldn't tell you why."

"Indeed," said Ehrengraf.

"You'll have some more tea, Mr. Ehrengraf?"

"If I may."

She leaned forward, displaying an alluring portion of herself to Ehrengraf as she filled his cup from a Dresden teapot. Then she set the pot down and straightened up with a sigh.

"Poor Mrs. Protter," she said. "Death is so final."

"Given the present state of medical science."

"And poor Mr. Protter. Will he have to spend many years in prison, Mr. Ehrengraf?"

"Not with a proper defense. Tell me, Miss Mullane. Mrs. Protter accused her husband of having an affair with you. I wonder why she should have brought such an accusation."

"I'm sure I don't know."

"Of course you're a very attractive woman—"

"Do you really think so, Mr. Ehrengraf?"

"—and you live by yourself, and tongues will wag."

"I'm a respectable woman, Mr. Ehrengraf."

"I'm sure you are."

"And I would never have an affair with anyone who lived here in this building. Discretion, Mr. Ehrengraf, is very important to me."

"I sensed that, Miss Mullane." The little lawyer got to his feet, walked to the window. The afternoon was warm, and the strains of Latin music drifted up through the open window from the street below.

"Transistor radios," Agnes Mullane said. "They carry them everywhere."

"So they do. When Mrs. Protter made that accusation, Miss Mullane, her husband denied it."

"Why, I should hope so!"

"And he in turn accused her of carrying on with Mr. Gates. Have I said something funny, Miss Mullane?"

Agnes Mullane managed to control her laughter. "Mr. Gates is an artist," she said.

"A painter, I'm told. Would that canvas be one of his?"

"I'm afraid not. He paints abstracts. I prefer representational art myself, as you can see."

"And country music."

"I beg your pardon?"

"Nothing. You're sure Mr. Gates was not having an affair with Mrs. Protter?"

"Positive." Her brow clouded for an instant, then cleared completely. "No," she said, "Harry Gates would never have been involved with her. But what's the point, Mr. Ehrengraf? Are you trying to establish a defense of justifiable homicide? The unwritten law and all that?"

"Not exactly."

"Because I really don't think it would work, do you?"

"No," said Ehrengraf, "I don't suppose it would."

Miss Mullane leaned forward again, not to pour tea but with a similar effect. "It's so noble of you," she said, "donating your time for poor Mr. Protter."

"The court appointed me, Miss Mullane."

"Yes, but surely not all appointed attorneys work so hard on these cases, do they?"

"Perhaps not."

"That's what I thought." She ran her tongue over her lips. "Nobility is an attractive quality in a man," she said thoughtfully. "And I've always admired men who dress well, and who bear themselves elegantly."

Ehrengraf smiled. He was wearing a pale blue cashmere sport jacket over a Wedgwood blue shirt. His tie matched his jacket, with an intricate below-the-knot design in gold thread.

"A lovely jacket," Miss Mullane purred. She reached over, laid a hand on sleeve. "Cashmere," she said. "I love the feel of cashmere."

"Thank you."

"And gray flannel slacks. What a fine fabric. Come with me, Mr. Ehrengraf. I'll show you where to hang your things."

In the bedroom Miss Mullane paused to switch on the radio. Loretta Lynn was singing something about having been born a coal miner's daughter.

"My one weakness," Miss Mullane said, "or should I say one of my two weaknesses, along with a weakness for well-dressed men of noble character. I hope you don't mind country music, Mr. Ehrengraf?"

"Not at all," said Ehrengraf. "I find it soothing."

═

Several days later, when Arnold Protter was released from jail, Ehrengraf was there to meet him. "I want to shake your hand," he told him, extending his own. "You're a free man now, Mr. Protter. I only regret I played no greater part in securing your freedom."

Protter pumped the lawyer's hand enthusiastically. "Hey, listen," he said, "you're ace-high with me, Mr. Ehrengraf. You believed in me when nobody else did, including me myself. I'm just now trying to take all of this in. I tell you, I never would have dreamed Agnes Mullane killed my wife."

"It's something neither of us suspected, Mr. Protter."

"It's the craziest thing I ever heard of. Let me see if I got the drift of it straight. My Gretchen was carrying on with Gates after all. I thought it was just a way to get in a dig at her, accusing her of carrying on with him, but actually it was happening all the time."

"So it would seem."

"And that's why she got so steamed when I brought it up." Protter nodded, wrapped up in thought. "Anyway, Gates also had something going with Agnes Mullane. You know something, Mr. Ehrengraf? He musta been nuts. Why would anybody who was getting next to Agnes want to bother with Gretchen?"

"Artists perceive the world differently from the rest of us, Mr. Protter."

"If that's a polite way of saying he was cockeyed, I sure gotta go with you on that. So here he's getting it on with the both of them, and Agnes finds out and she's jealous. How do you figure she found out?"

"It's always possible Gates told her," Ehrengraf suggested. "Or perhaps she heard you accusing your wife of infidelity. You and Gretchen had both been drinking, and your argument may have been a loud one."

"Could be. A few boilermakers and I tend to raise my voice."

"Most people do. Or perhaps Miss Mullane saw some of Gates's sketches of your wife. I understand there were several found in his apartment. He may have been an abstract expressionist, but he seems to have been capable of realistic sketches of nudes. Of course he's denied they were his work, but he'd be likely to say that, wouldn't he?"

"I guess so," Protter said. "Naked pictures of Gretchen, gee, you never know, do you?"

"You never do," Ehrengraf agreed. "In any event, Miss Mullane had a key to your apartment. One was found among her effects. Perhaps it was Gates's key, perhaps Gretchen had given it to him and Agnes Mullane stole it. She let herself into your apartment, found you and your wife unconscious, and pounded your wife on the head with an empty beer bottle. Your wife was alive when Miss Mullane entered your apartment, Mr. Protter, and dead when she left it."

"So I didn't kill her after all."

"Indeed you did not." Ehrengraf smiled for a moment. Then his face turned grave. "Agnes Mullane was not cut out for murder," he said. "At heart she was a gentle soul. I realized that at once when I spoke with her."

"You went and talked to Agnes?"

The little lawyer nodded. "I suspect my interview with her may have driven her over the edge," he said. "Perhaps she sensed that I was suspicious of her. She wrote out a letter to the police, detailing what she had done. Then she must have gone upstairs to Mr. Gates's apartment, because she managed to secure a twenty-five caliber automatic pistol registered to him. She returned to her own apartment, put the weapon to her chest, and shot herself in the heart."

"She had some chest, too."

Ehrengraf did not comment.

"I'll tell you," Protter said, "the whole thing's a little too complicated for a simple guy like me to take it all in all at once. I can see why it was open and shut as far as the cops were concerned. There's me and the wife drinking, and there's me and the wife fighting, and the next thing you know she's dead and I'm sleeping it off. If it wasn't for you, I'd be doing time for killing her."

"I played a part," Ehrengraf said modestly. "But it's Agnes Mullane's conscience that saved you from prison."

"Poor Agnes."

"A tortured, tormented woman, Mr. Protter."

"I don't know about that," Protter said. "But she had some body on her, I'll say that for her." He drew a breath. "What about you, Mr. Ehrengraf? You did a real job for me. I wish I could pay you."

"Don't worry about it."

"I guess the court pays you something, huh?"

"There's a set fee of a hundred and seventy-five dollars," Ehrengraf said, "but I don't know that I'm eligible to receive it in this instance because of the disposition of the case. The argument may be raised that I didn't really perform any actions on your behalf, that charges were simply dropped."

"You mean you'll get gypped out of your fee? That's a hell of a note, Mr. Ehrengraf."

"Oh, don't worry about it," said Ehrengraf. "It's not important in the overall scheme of things."

≡

Ehrengraf, his blue pinstripe suit setting off his Caedmon Society striped necktie, sipped daintily at a Calvados. It was Indian summer this afternoon, far too balmy for hot apple pie with cheddar cheese. He was eating instead a piece of cold apple pie topped with vanilla ice cream, and had discovered that Calvados went every bit as nicely with that dish.

Across from him, Hudson Cutliffe sat with a plate of lamb stew. When Cutliffe had ordered the dish, Ehrengraf had refrained from commenting on the barbarity of slaughtering lambs and stewing them. He had decided to ignore the contents of Cutliffe's plate. Whatever he'd ordered, Ehrengraf intended that the man eat crow today.

"You," said Cutliffe, "are the most astonishingly fortunate lawyer who ever passed the bar."

"'Dame Fortune is a fickle gypsy, And always blind, and often tipsy,'" Ehrengraf quoted. "Winthrop Mackworth Praed, born eighteen-oh-two, died eighteen thirty-nine. But you don't care for poetry, do you? Perhaps you'd prefer the elder Pliny's observation upon the eruption of Vesuvius. He said that Fortune favors the brave."

"A cliché, isn't it?"

"Perhaps it was rather less a cliché when Pliny said it," Ehrengraf said gently. "But that's beside the point. My client was innocent, just as I told you—"

"How on earth could you have known it?"

"I didn't have to know it. I presumed it, Mr. Cutliffe, as I always presume my clients to be innocent, and as in time they are invariably proven to be. And, because you were so incautious as to insist upon a wager—"

"Insist!"

"It was indeed your suggestion," Ehrengraf said. "*I* did not seek *you* out, Mr. Cutliffe. *I* did not seat myself unbidden at *your* table."

"You came to this restaurant," Cutliffe said darkly. "You deliberately baited me, goaded me. You—"

"Oh, come now," Ehrengraf said. "You make me sound like what priests would call an occasion of sin or lawyers an attractive nuisance. I came here for apple pie with cheese, Mr. Cutliffe, and you proposed a wager. Now my client has been released and all charges dropped, and I believe you owe me money."

"It's not as if you got him off. Fate got him off."

Ehrengraf rolled his eyes. "Oh, please, Mr. Cutliffe," he said. "I've had clients take that stance, you know, and they change their minds in the end. My agreement with them has always been that my fee is due and payable upon their release, whether the case comes to court or not, whether or not I have played any evident part in their salvation. I specified precisely those terms when we arranged our little wager."

"Of course gambling debts are not legally collectible in this state."

"Of course they are not, Mr. Cutliffe. Yours is purely a debt of honor, an attribute which you may or may not be said to possess in accordance with your willingness to write out a check. But I trust you are an honorable man, Mr. Cutliffe."

Their eyes met. After a long moment Cutliffe drew a checkbook from his pocket. "I feel I've been manipulated in some devious fashion," he said, "but at the same time I can't gloss over the fact that I owe you money." He opened the checkbook, uncapped a pen, and filled out the check quickly, signing it with a flourish. Ehrengraf smiled narrowly, placing the check in his own wallet without noting the amount. It was, let it be said, an impressive amount.

"An astonishing case," Cutliffe said, "even if you yourself had the smallest of parts in it. This morning's news was the most remarkable thing of all."

"Oh?"

"I'm referring to Gates's confession, of course."

"Gates's confession?"

"You haven't heard? Oh, this is rich. Harry Gates is in jail. He went to the police and confessed to murdering Gretchen Protter."

"Gates murdered Gretchen Protter?"

"No question about it. It seems he shot her, used the very same small-caliber automatic pistol that the Mullane woman stole and used to kill herself. He was having an affair with both the women, just as Agnes Mullane said in her suicide note. He heard Protter accuse his wife of infidelity and was afraid Agnes Mullane would find out he'd been carrying on with Gretchen Protter. So he went down there looking to clear the air, and he had the gun along for protection, and—are you sure you didn't know about this?"

"Keep talking," Ehrengraf urged.

"Well, he found the two of them out cold. At first he thought Gretchen was dead but he saw she was breathing, and he took a raw potato from the refrigerator and used it as a silencer, and he shot Gretchen in the heart. They never found the bullet during postmortem examination because they weren't looking for it, just assumed massive skull injuries had caused her death. But after he confessed they looked, and there was the bullet right where he said it should be, and Gates is in jail charged with her murder."

"Why on earth did he confess?"

"He was in love with Agnes Mullane," Cutliffe said. "That's why he killed Gretchen. Then Agnes Mullane killed herself, taking the blame for a crime Gates committed, and he cracked wide open. Figures her death was some sort of divine retribution, and he has to clear things by paying the price for the Protter woman's death. The D.A. thinks perhaps he killed them both, faked Agnes Mullane's confession note, and then couldn't win the battle with his own conscience. He insists he didn't, of course, as he insists he didn't draw nude sketches of either of the women, but it seems there's some question now about the validity of Agnes Mullane's suicide note, so it may well turn out that Gates killed her, too. Because if Gates killed Gretchen, why would Agnes have committed suicide?"

"I'm sure there are any number of possible explanations," Ehrengraf said, his fingers worrying the tips of his trimmed mustache. "Any number of explanations. Do you know the epitaph Andrew Marvell wrote for a lady?

"To say—she lived a virgin chaste
In this age loose and all unlaced;
Nor was, when vice is so allowed,
Of virtue or ashamed or proud;
That her soul was on Heaven so bent,
No minute but it came and went;
That, ready her last debt to pay,

She summed her life every day;
Modest as morn, as mid-day bright,
Gentle as evening, cool as night:
—'Tis true; but all too weakly said;
'Twas more significant, she's dead.

"She's dead, Mr. Cutliffe, and we may leave her to heaven, as another poet has said. My client was innocent. That's the only truly relevant point. My client was innocent."

"As you somehow knew all along."

"As I knew all along, yes. Yes, indeed, as I knew all along." Ehrengraf's fingers drummed the tabletop. "Perhaps you could get our waiter's eye," he suggested. "I think I might enjoy another glass of Calvados."

The EHRENGRAF Riposte

"Let Ross, house of Ross, rejoice with Obadiah, and the rankle-dankle fish with hands."

—Christopher Smart

Martin Ehrengraf placed his hands on the top of his exceedingly cluttered desk and looked across it. He was seated, while the man at whom he gazed was standing, and indeed looked incapable of remaining still, let alone seating himself on a chair. He was a large man, tall and quite stout, balding, florid of face, with a hawk's-bill nose and a jutting chin. His hair, combed straight back, was a rich and glossy dark brown; his bushy eyebrows were salted with gray. His suit, while of a particular shade of blue that Ehrengraf would never have chosen for himself, was well tailored and expensive. It was logical to assume that the man within the suit was abundantly supplied with money, an assumption the little lawyer liked to be able to make about all his prospective clients.

Now he said, "Won't you take a seat, Mr. Crowe? You'll be more comfortable."

"I'd rather stand," Ethan Crowe said. "I'm too much on edge to sit still."

"Hmmm. There's something I've learned in my practice, Mr. Crowe, and that's the great advantage in acting *as if.* When I'm to defend a client who gives every indication of guilt, I act *as if* he were indeed innocent.

And you know, Mr. Crowe, it's astonishing how often the client does in fact *prove* to be innocent, often to his own surprise."

Martin Ehrengraf flashed a smile that showed on his lips without altering the expression in his eyes. "All of which is all-important to me, since I collect a fee only if my client is judged to be innocent. Otherwise I go unpaid. Acting *as if*, Mr. Crowe, is uncannily helpful, and you might help us both by sitting in that chair and acting as if you were at peace with the world."

Ehrengraf paused, and when Crowe had seated himself he said, "You say you've been charged with murder. But homicide is not usually a bailable offense, so how does it happen that you are here in my office instead of locked in a cell?"

"I haven't been charged with murder."

"But you said—"

"I said I wanted you to defend me against a homicide charge. But I haven't been charged yet."

"I see. Whom have you killed? Let me amend that. Whom are you supposed to have killed?"

"No one."

"Oh?"

Ethan Crowe thrust his head forward. "I'll be charged with the murder of Terence Reginald Mayhew," he said, pronouncing the name with a full measure of loathing. "But I haven't been charged yet because the rancid scut's not dead yet because I haven't killed him yet."

"Mr. Mayhew is alive."

'Yes."

"But you intend to kill him."

Crowe chose his words carefully. "I expect to be charged with his murder," he said at length.

"And you want to arrange your defense in advance."

"Yes."

"You show commendable foresight," Ehrengraf said admiringly. He got to his feet and stepped out from behind his desk. He was a muted symphony of brown. His jacket was a brown Harris tweed in a herringbone weave, his slacks were cocoa flannel, his shirt a buttery tan silk, his tie a perfect match for the slacks with a below-the-knot design of fleur-de-lis in silver thread. Ehrengraf hadn't been quite certain about the tie when he bought it but had since decided it was quite all right. On his small feet he wore highly polished seamless tan loafers, unadorned with braids or tassels.

"Foresight," he repeated. "An unusual quality in a client, Mr. Crowe, and I can only wish that I met with it more frequently." He put the tips of his fingers together and narrowed his eyes. "Just what is it you wish from me?"

"Your efforts on my behalf, of course."

"Indeed. Why do you want to kill Mr. Mayhew?"

"Because he's driving me crazy."

"How?"

"He's playing tricks on me."

"Tricks? What sort of tricks?"

"Childish tricks," Ethan Crowe said, and averted his eyes. "He makes phone calls. He orders things. Last week he called different florists and sent out hundreds of orders of flowers to different women all over the city. He's managed to get hold of my credit card numbers, and he placed all these orders in my name and billed them to me. I was able to stop some of the orders, but by the time I got wind of what he'd done, most of them had already gone out."

"Surely you won't have to pay."

"It may be easier to pay than to go through the process of avoiding payment. I don't know. But that's just one example. Another time ambulances and limousines kept coming to my house. One after the other. And taxicabs, and I don't know what else. These vehicles kept arriving from various sources and I kept having to send them away."

"I see."

"And he fills out coupons and orders things C.O.D. for me. I have to cancel the orders and return the products. He's had me join book clubs and record clubs, he's subscribed me to every sort of magazine, he's put me on every sort of mailing list. Did you know, for example, that there's an outfit called the International Society for the Preservation of Wild Mustangs and Burros?"

"It so happens I'm a member."

"Well, I'm sure it's a worthwhile organization," Crowe said, "but the point is I'm not interested in wild mustangs and burros, or even tame ones, but Mayhew made me a member and pledged a hundred dollars on my behalf, or maybe it was a thousand dollars, I can't remember."

"The exact amount isn't important at the moment, Mr. Crowe."

"He's driving me crazy!"

"So it would seem. But to kill a man because of some practical jokes—"

"There's no end to them. He started doing this almost two years ago. At first it was completely maddening because I had no idea what was happening or who was doing this to me. From time to time he'll slack off and I'll think he's had his fun and has decided to leave me alone. Then he'll start up again."

"Have you spoken to him?"

"I can't. He laughs like the lunatic he is and hangs up on me."

"Have you confronted him?"

"I can't. He lives in an apartment downtown on Chippewa Street. He doesn't let visitors in and never seems to leave the place."

"And you've tried the police?"

"They can't seem to do anything. He just lies to them, denies all responsibility, tells them it must be someone else. A very nice policeman told me the only sensible thing I can do is wait him out. He'll get tired, he assured me, the man's madness will run its course. He'll decide he's had his revenge."

"And you tried to do that?"

"For a while. When it didn't work, I engaged a private detective. He obtained evidence of activities, evidence that will stand up in court. But attorney convinced me not to press charges."

"Why, for heaven's sake?"

"The man's a cripple."

"Your attorney?"

"Certainly not. Mayhew's a cripple, he's confined to a wheelchair. I suppose that's why he never leaves his squalid little apartment. But my attorney said I could only charge him with malicious mischief, which is not the most serious crime in the book and which sounds rather less serious than it is because it has the connotation of a child's impish prank—"

"Yes."

"—and there we'd be in court, myself a large man in good physical condition and Mayhew a sniveling cripple in a wheelchair, and he'd get everyone's sympathy and undoubtedly be exonerated of all charges while I'd come off as a bully and a laughingstock. I couldn't make charges stand up in criminal court, and if I sued him I'd probably lose. And even if I won, what could I possibly collect? The man doesn't have anything to start with."

Ehrengraf nodded thoughtfully. "He blames you for crippling him?"

"I can't imagine why. I had never even heard of him before he started tormenting me, but who knows what a madman might think? He doesn't seem to want anything from me. I've called him up, asked him what he wanted, and he laughs and hangs up on me."

"And so you've decided to kill him."

"I haven't said that."

Ehrengraf sighed. "We're not in court, Mr. Crowe, so that sort of technicality's not important between us. You've implied you intend to kill him."

"Perhaps."

"At any rate, that's the inference I've drawn. I can certainly understand your feelings, but isn't the remedy you propose an extreme one? The cure seems worse than the disease. To expose yourself to a murder trial—"

"But your clients rarely go to trial." Crowe said, and hazarded a smile. It looked out of place on his large red face, and after a moment it withdrew. "I'm familiar with your methods, Mr. Ehrengraf," he went on. "Your clients rarely go to trial. You hardly ever show up in a courtroom. You take a case and then something curious happens. The evidence changes, or new evidence is discovered, or someone else confesses, or the murder turns out to be an accident, after all, or—well, *something* always happens."

"Truth will out," Ehrengraf said.

"Truth or fiction, something happens. Now here I am, plagued by a maniac, and I've engaged you to undertake my defense whenever it should become necessary, and it seems to me that by so doing I may bring things to the point where it *won't* become necessary."

Ehrengraf looked at him. A man who would select a suit of that particular shade, he thought, was either color blind or capable of anything.

"Of course I don't know what might happen," Ethan Crowe went on. "Just as hypothesis, Terence might die. Of course, if that happened I wouldn't have any reason to murder him, and so I wouldn't come to trial. But that's just an example. It's certainly not my business to tell you your business, is it?"

"Certainly not," said Martin Ehrengraf.

≡

While Terence Reginald Mayhew's four-room apartment on Chippewa Street was scarcely luxurious, it was by no means the squalid pesthole Ehrengraf had been led to expect. The block, to be sure, was not far removed from slum status. The building itself had certainly seen better days. But the Mayhew apartment itself, occupying the fourth-floor front and looking northward over a group of two-story frame houses, was cozy and comfortable.

The little lawyer followed Mayhew's wheelchair down a short hallway and into a book-lined study. A log of wax and compressed sawdust burned in the fireplace. A clock ticked on the mantel. Mayhew turned his wheelchair around, eyed his visitor from head to toe, and made a brisk clucking sound with his tongue. "So you're his lawyer," he said. "Not the poor boob who called me a couple of months ago, though. That one kept coming up with threats and I couldn't help laughing at him. He must have turned purple. When you laugh in a man's face after he's made legal threats, he generally turns purple. That's been my experience. What's your name again?"

"Ehrengraf. Martin H. Ehrengraf."

"What's the H. stand for?"

"Harrod."

"Like the king in the Bible?"

"Like the London department store." Ehrengraf's middle name was not Harrod, or Herod either, for that matter. He simply found untruths useful now and then, particularly in response to impertinence.

"Martin Harrod Ehrengraf," said Terence Reginald Mayhew. "Well, you're quite the dandy, aren't you? Sorry the place isn't spiffier but the cleaning woman only comes in once a week and she's not due until the day after. Not that she's any great shakes with a dustcloth. Lazy slattern, in my opinion. You want to sit down?"

"No."

"Probably scared to crease your pants."

Ehrengraf was wearing a navy suit, a pale-blue velvet vest, a blue shirt, a knit tie, and a pair of cordovan loafers. Mayhew was wearing a disgraceful terrycloth robe and tatty bedroom slippers. He had a scrawny body, a volleyball-shaped head, big guileless blue eyes, and red straw for hair. He was not so much ugly as bizarre; he looked like a cartoonist's invention. Ehrengraf couldn't guess how old he was—thirty? forty? fifty?—but it didn't matter. The man was years from dying of old age.

"Well, aren't you going to threaten me?"

"No," Ehrengraf said.

"No threats? No hint of bodily harm? No pending lawsuits? No criminal prosecution?"

"Nothing of the sort."

"Well, you're an improvement on your predecessor," Mayhew said. "That's something. Why'd you come here, then? Not to see how the rich folks live. You slumming?"

"No."

"Because it may be a rundown neighborhood, but it's a good apartment. They'd get me out if they could. Rent control—I've been here for ages and my rent's a pittance. Never find anything like this for what I can afford to pay. I get checks every month, you see. Disability. Small trust fund. Doesn't add up to much, but I get by. Have the cleaning woman in once a week, pay the rent, eat decent food. Watch the TV, read my books and magazines, play my chess games by mail. Neighborhood's gone down but I don't live in the neighborhood. I live in the apartment. All I get of the neighborhood is seeing it from my window, and if it's not fancy that's all right with me. I'm a cripple, I'm confined to these four rooms, so what do I care what the neighborhood's like? If I was blind I wouldn't care what color the walls were painted, would I? The more they take away from you, why, the less vulnerable you are."

That last was an interesting thought and Ehrengraf might have pursued it, but he had other things to pursue. "My client," he said. "Ethan Crowe."

"That warthog."

"You dislike him?"

"Stupid question, Mr. Lawyer. Of course I dislike him. I wouldn't keep putting the wind up him if I thought the world of him, would I now?"

"You blame him for—"

"For me being a cripple? He didn't do that to me. God did." The volleyball head bounced against the back of the wheelchair, the wide slash of mouth opened and a cackle of laughter spilled out. "God did it! I was born this way, you chowderhead. Ethan Crowe had nothing to do with it."

"Then—"

"I just hate the man," Mayhew said. "Who needs a reason? I saw a preacher on Sunday-morning television; he stared right into the camera every minute with those great big eyes, said no one has cause to hate his fellow man. At first it made me want to retch, but I thought about it, and I'll be an anthropoid ape if he's not right. No one has cause to hate his fellow man because no one *needs* cause to hate his fellow man. It's natural. And it comes natural for me to hate Ethan Crowe."

"Have you ever met him?"

"I don't have to meet him."

"You just—"

"I just hate him," Mayhew said, grinning fiercely, "and I love hating him, and I have heaps of *fun* hating him, and all I have to do is pick up that phone and make him pay and pay and pay for it."

"Pay for what?"

"For everything. For being Ethan Crowe. For the outstanding war debt. For the loaves and the fishes." The head bounced back and the insane laugh was repeated. "For Tippecanoe and Tyler, too. For Tippecanee and Tyler Three."

"You don't have very much money," Ehrengraf said. "A disability pension, a small income."

"I have enough. I don't eat much and I don't eat fancy. You probably spend more on clothes than I spend on everything put together."

Ehrengraf didn't doubt that for a moment. "My client might supplement that income of yours," he said thoughtfully.

"You think I'm a blackmailer?"

"I think you might profit by circumstances, Mr. Mayhew."

"Fie on it, sir. I'd have no truck with blackmail. The Mayhews have been whitemailers for generations."

The conversation continued, but not for long. It became quite clear to the diminutive attorney that his was a limited arsenal. He could neither threaten nor bribe to any purpose. Any number of things might happen to Mayhew, some of them fatal, but such action seemed wildly disproportionate. This housebound wretch, this malevolent cripple, had simply not done enough to warrant such a response. When a child thumbed his nose at you, you were not supposed to dash its brains out against the curb. An action ought to bring about a suitable reaction. A thrust should be countered with an appropriate riposte.

But how was one to deal with a nasty madman? A helpless, pathetic madman?

Ehrengraf, who was fond of poetry, sought his memory for an illuminating phrase. Thoughts of madmen recalled Christopher Smart, an eighteenth-century poet who was periodically confined to Bedlam where he wrote a long poem that was largely comprehensible only to himself and God.

Quoting Smart, Ehrengraf said, "'Let Ross, house of Ross, rejoice with Obadiah, and the rankle-dankle fish with hands.'"

Terence Reginald Mayhew nodded. "Now that," he said, "is the first sensible thing you've said since you walked in here."

≡

A dozen days later, while Martin Ehrengraf was enjoying a sonnet of Thomas Hood's, his telephone rang. He took it up, said hello, and heard himself called an unconscionable swine.

"Ah," he said. "Mr. Mayhew."

"You are a man with no heart. I'm a poor housebound cripple, Mr. Ehrengraf—"

"Indeed."

"—and you've taken my life away. Do you have any notion what I had to go through to make this phone call?"

"I have a fair idea."

"Do you have any idea what I've been going through?"

"A fair idea of that as well," Ehrengraf said. "Here's a pretty coincidence. Just as you called, I was reading this poem of Thomas Hood's—do you know him?"

"I don't know what you're talking about."

"A sonnet called *Silence*. I'll just read you the sestet:

> "But in green ruins, in the desolate walls,
> Of antique palaces, where Man hath been,
> Though the dun fox or wild hyena calls,
> And owls that flit continually between,
> Shriek to the echo, and the low winds moan—
> There the true silence is, self-conscious and alone.

"Don't you think that's marvelously evocative of what you've been going through, Mr. Mayhew?"

"You're a terrible man."

"Indeed. And you should never forget it."

"I won't."

"It could all happen again. In fact, it could happen over and over."

"What do I have to do?"

"You have to leave my client strictly alone."

"I was having so much *fun*."

"Don't whine, Mr. Mayhew. You can't play your nasty little tricks on Mr. Crowe. But there's a whole world of other victims out there just waiting for your attentions."

"You mean—"

"I'm sure I've said nothing that wouldn't have occurred to you in good time, sir. On the other hand, you never know what some other victim might do. He might even find his way to my office, and you know full well what the consequences of that would be. Indeed, you know that you *can't* know. So perhaps what you ought to do is grow up, Mr. Mayhew, and wrap the tattered scraps of your life around your wretched body, and make the best of it."

"I don't—"

"Think of Thomas Hood, sir. Think of the true silence."

"I can't—"

"Think of Ross, house of Ross, and the rankle-dankle fish with hands."

"I'm not—"

"And think of Mr. Crowe while you're at it. I suggest you call him, sir. Apologize to him. Assure him that his troubles are over."

"I don't want to call him."

"Make the call," Ehrengraf said, his voice smooth as steel. "Or your troubles, Mr. Mayhew, are just beginning."

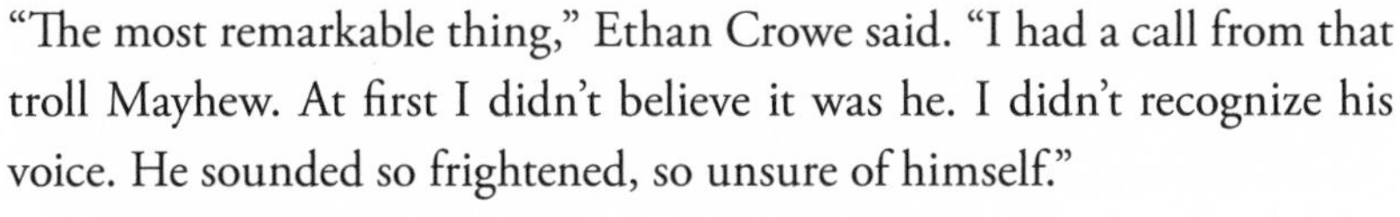

"The most remarkable thing," Ethan Crowe said. "I had a call from that troll Mayhew. At first I didn't believe it was he. I didn't recognize his voice. He sounded so frightened, so unsure of himself."

"Indeed."

"He assured me I'd have no further trouble from him. No more limousines or taxis, no more flowers, none of his idiotic little pranks. He apologized profusely for all the trouble he'd caused me in the past and assured me it would never happen again. It's hard to know whether to take the word of a madman, but I think he meant what he said."

"I'm certain he did."

They were once again in Martin Ehrengraf's office, and as usual the lawyer's desk was as cluttered as his person was immaculate. He was wearing the navy suit again, as it happened, but he had left the light-blue vest at home. His tie bore a half-inch diagonal stripe of royal blue flanked by two narrower stripes, one of gold and the other of a rather bright green, all on a navy field. Crowe was wearing a three-piece suit, expensive and beautifully tailored but in a rather morose shade of brown. Ehrengraf had decided charitably to regard the man as color blind and let it go at that.

"What did you do, Ehrengraf?"

The little lawyer looked off into the middle distance. "I suppose I can tell you," he said after a moment's reflection. "I took his life away from him."

"That's what I thought you would do. Take his life, I mean. But he was certainly alive when I spoke to him."

"You misunderstand me. Mr. Crowe, your antagonist was a house-bound cripple who had adjusted to his mean little life of isolation. He had an income sufficient to his meager needs. And I went around his house shutting things down."

"I don't understand."

"I speak metaphorically, of course. Well, there's no reason I can't tell you what I did in plain English. First of all, I went to the post office. I filled out a change-of-address card, signed it in his name, and filed it. From that moment on, all his mail was efficiently forwarded to the General Delivery window in Greeley, Colorado, where it's to be held until called for, which may take rather a long time."

"Good heavens."

"I notified the electric company that Mr. Mayhew had vacated the premises and ordered them to cut off service forthwith. I told the telephone company the same thing, so when he picked up the phone to complain about the lights being out I'm afraid he had a hard time getting a dial tone. I sent a notarized letter to the landlord—over Mr. Mayhew's signature, of course—announcing that he was moving and demanding that his lease be canceled. I got in touch with his cleaning woman and informed her that her services would no longer be required. I could go on, Mr. Crowe, but I believe you get the idea. I took his life away and shut it down and he didn't like it."

"Good grief."

"His only remaining contact with the world was what he saw through his windows, and that was nothing attractive. Nevertheless, I was going to have his windows painted black from the outside—I was in the process of making final arrangements. A chap was going to suspend a scaffold as if to wash the windows but he would have painted them instead. I saw it as a neat coup de grace, but Mayhew made that last touch unnecessary by throwing in the sponge. That's a mixed metaphor, from coup de grace to throwing in the sponge, but I hope you'll pardon it."

"You did to him what he'd done to me. Hoist him on his own petard."

"Let's say I hoisted him on a similar petard. He plagued you by introducing an infinity of unwanted elements into your life. But I reduced his life to the four rooms he lived in and even threatened his ability to retain those very rooms. That drove the lesson home to him in a way I doubt he'll ever forget."

"Simple and brilliant," Crowe said. "I wish I'd thought of it."

"I'm glad you didn't."

"Why?"

"Because you'd have saved yourself fifty thousand dollars."

Crowe gasped. "Fifty thousand—"

"Dollars. My fee."

"But that's an outrage. All you did was write some letters and make some phone calls."

"All I did, sir, was everything you asked me to do. I saved you from answering to a murder charge."

"I wouldn't have murdered him."

"Nonsense," Ehrengraf snapped. "You *tried* to murder him. You thought engaging me would have precisely that effect. Had I wrung the wretch's neck you'd pay my fee without a whimper, but because I accomplished the desired result with style and grace instead of brute force you now resist paying me. It would be an immense act of folly, Mr. Crowe, if you were to do anything other than pay my fee in full at once."

'You don't think the amount is out of line?"

"I don't keep my fees in a line, Mr. Crowe." Ehrengraf's hand went to the knot of his tie. It was the official necktie of the Caedmon Society of Oxford University. Ehrengraf had not attended Oxford and did not belong to the Caedmon Society any more than he belonged to the International Society for the Preservation of Wild Mustangs and Burros, but it was a tie he habitually wore on celebratory occasions. "I set my fees according to an intuitive process," he went on, "and they are never negotiable. Fifty thousand dollars, sir. Not a penny more, not a penny less. Ah, Mr. Crowe, Mr. Crowe—do you know why Mayhew chose to torment you?"

"I suppose he feels I've harmed him."

"And have you?"

"No, but—"

"Supposition is blunder's handmaiden, Mr. Crowe. Mayhew made your life miserable because he hated you. I don't know why he hated you. I don't believe Mayhew himself knows why he hated you. I think he selected you at random. He needed someone to hate and you were convenient. Ah, Mr. Crowe—" Ehrengraf smiled with his lips "—consider how much damage was done to you by an insane cripple with no actual reason to do you harm. And then consider, sir, how much more harm could be done you by someone infinitely more ruthless and resourceful than Terence Reginald Mayhew, someone who is neither a lunatic nor a cripple, someone who is supplied with fifty thousand excellent reasons to wish you ill."

Crowe stared. "That's a threat," he said slowly.

"I fear you've confused a threat and a caution, Mr. Crowe, though I warrant the distinction's a thin one. Are you fond of poetry, sir?"

"No."

"I'm not surprised. It's no criticism, sir. Some people have poetry in their souls and others do not. It's predetermined, I suspect, like color blindness. I could recommend Thomas Hood, sir, or Christopher Smart, but would you read them? Or profit by them? Fifty thousand dollars, Mr. Crowe, and a check will do nicely."

"I'm not afraid of you."

"Certainly not."

"And I won't be intimidated."

"Indeed you won't," Ehrengraf agreed. "But do you recall our initial interview, Mr. Crowe? I submit that you would do well to act *as if*—as if you were afraid of me, as if you were intimidated."

Ethan Crowe sat quite still for several seconds. A variety of expressions played over his generally unexpressive face. At length he drew a checkbook from the breast pocket of his morosely brown jacket and uncapped a silver fountain pen.

"Payable to?"

"Martin H. Ehrengraf."

The pen scratched away. Then, idly, "What's the H. stand for?"

"Herod."

"The store in England?"

"The king," said Ehrengraf. "The king in the Bible."

The EHRENGRAF Obligation

"Play me songs with flatted thirds:
Puppets dance from bloody strings.
Music mourns dead birds.
Breath is sweet in broken things."

—William Telliford

William Telliford gave his head a tentative scratch, in part because it itched, in part out of puzzlement. It itched because he had been unable to wash his lank brown hair during the four days he'd thus far spent in jail. He was puzzled because this dapper man before him was proposing to get him out of jail.

"I don't understand," he said. "The court appointed an attorney for me. A younger man, I think he said his name was Trabner. You're not associated with him or anything, are you?"

"Certainly not."

"Your name is—"

"Martin Ehrengraf."

"Well, I appreciate your coming to see me, Mr. Ehrengraf, but I've already got a lawyer, this Mr. Trabner, and—"

"Are you satisfied with Mr. Trabner?"

Telliford lowered his eyes, focusing his gaze upon the little lawyer's shoes, a pair of highly polished black wing tips. "I suppose he's all right," he said slowly.

"But?"

"But he doesn't believe I'm innocent. I mean he seems to take it for granted I'm guilty and the best thing I can do is plead guilty to manslaughter or something. He's talking in terms of making some kind of deal with the district attorney, like it's a foregone conclusion that I have to go to prison and the only question is how long."

"Then you've answered my question," Ehrengraf said, a smile flickering on his thin lips. "You're unsatisfied with your lawyer. The court has appointed him. It remains for you to disappoint him, as it were, and to engage me in his stead. You have the right to do this, you know."

"But I don't have the money. Trabner was going to defend me for free, which is about as much as I can afford. I don't know what kind of fees you charge for something like this but I'll bet they're substantial. That suit of yours didn't come from the Salvation Army."

Ehrengraf beamed. His suit, charcoal gray flannel with a nipped-in waist, had been made for him by a most exclusive tailor. His shirt was pink, with a button-down collar. His vest was a Tattersall check, red and black on a cream background, and his tie showed half-inch stripes of red and charcoal gray. "My fees are on the high side," he allowed. "To undertake your defense I would ordinarily set a fee of eighty thousand dollars."

"Eighty dollars would strain my budget," William Telliford said. "Eighty thousand, well, it might take me ten years to earn that much."

"But I propose to defend free of charge, sir."

William Telliford stared, not least because he could not recall the last time anyone had thought to call him sir. He was, it must be said, a rather unprepossessing young man, much given to slouching and sprawling. His jeans needed patching at the knees. His plaid flannel shirt needed washing and ironing. His chukka boots needed soles and heels, and his socks needed replacement altogether.

"But—"

"But why?"

Telliford nodded.

"Because you are a poet," said Martin Ehrengraf. "And poets, as I'm sure you recall, are the unacknowledged legislators of the universe."

THE EHRENGRAF Obligation

"That's beautiful," Robin Littlefield said. She didn't know just what to make of this little man but he was certainly impressive. "Could you say that again? I want to remember it."

"Poets are the unacknowledged legislators of the universe. But don't credit me with the observation. Shelley said it first."

"Is she your wife?"

The deeply set dark eyes narrowed perceptibly. "Percy Bysshe Shelley," he said gently. "Born 1792, died 1822. The poet."

"Oh."

"So your young man is one of the world's unacknowledged legislators. Or you might prefer the lines Arthur O'Shaughnessy wrote. 'We are the music makers, And we are the dreamers of dreams.' You know the poem?"

"I don't think so."

"I like the second stanza," said Ehrengraf, and tilted his head to one side and quoted it:

> "With wonderful deathless ditties
> We build up the world's greatest cities,
> And out of a fabulous story
> We fashion an empire's glory:
> One man with a dream, at pleasure,
> Shall go forth and conquer a crown;
> And three with a new song's measure
> Can trample an empire down."

"You have a wonderful way of speaking. But I, uh, I don't really know much about poetry."

"You reserve your enthusiasm for Mr. Telliford's poems, no doubt."

"Well, I like it when Bill reads them to me. I like the way they sound, but I'll be the first to admit I don't always know what he's getting at."

Ehrengraf beamed, spread his hands. "But they do sound good, don't they? Miss Littlefield, dare we require more of a poem than that it please our ears? I don't read much modern poetry, Miss Littlefield. I prefer the bards of an earlier and more innocent age. Their verses are often simpler, but I don't pretend to understand any number of favorite poems. Half the time I couldn't tell you just what Blake's getting at, Miss Littlefield, but that doesn't keep me from enjoying his work. That sonnet of your young man's, that poem about riding a train across Kansas and looking at the moon. I'm sure you remember it."

"Sort of."

"He writes of the moon 'stroking desperate tides in the liquid land.' That's a lovely line, Miss Littlefield, and who cares whether the poem itself is fully comprehensible? Who'd raise such a niggling point? William Telliford is a poet and I'm under an obligation to defend him. I'm certain he couldn't have murdered that woman."

Robin gnawed a thumbnail. "The police are pretty sure he did it," she said. "The fire axe was missing from the hallway of our building and the glass case where it was kept was smashed open. And Janice Penrose, he used to live with her before he met me, well, they say he was still going around her place sometimes when I was working at the diner. And they never found the fire axe, but Bill came home with his jeans and shirt covered with blood and couldn't remember what happened. And he was seen in her neighborhood, and he'd been drinking, plus he smoked a lot of dope that afternoon and he was always taking pills. Ups and downs, like, plus some green capsules he stole from somebody's medicine chest and we were never quite sure what they were, but they do weird things to your head."

"The artist is so often the subject of his own experiment," Ehrengraf said sympathetically. "Think of De Quincey. Consider Coleridge, waking from an opium dream with all of 'Kubla Khan' fixed in his mind, just waiting for him to write it down. Of course he was interrupted by that dashed man from Porlock, but the lines he did manage to save are so wonderful. You know the poem, Miss Littlefield?"

"I think we had to read it in school."

"Perhaps."

"Or didn't he write something about an albatross? Some guy shot an albatross, something like that."

"Something like that."

═══

"The thing is," William Telliford said, "the more I think about it, the more I come to the conclusion that I must have killed Jan. I mean, who else would kill her?"

"You're innocent," Ehrengraf told him.

"You really think so? I can't remember what happened that day. I was doing some drugs and hitting the wine pretty good, and then I found this bottle of bourbon that I didn't think we still had, and I started drinking that, and that's about the last thing I remember. I must have gone right into blackout and the next thing I knew I was walking around covered with blood. And I've got a way of being violent when I'm drunk. When I lived with Jan I beat her up a few times, and I did the same with Robin. That's one of the reasons her father hates me."

"Her father hates you?"

"Despises me. Oh, I can't really blame him. He's this self-made man with more money than God and I'm squeezing by on food stamps. There's not much of a living in poetry."

"It's an outrage."

"Right. When Robin and I moved in together, well, her old man had a fit. Up to then he was laying a pretty heavy check on her the first of every month, but as soon as she moved in with me that was the end of that song. No more money for her. Here's her little brother going to this fancy private school and her mother dripping in sables and emeralds and diamonds and mink, and here's Robin slinging hash in a greasy spoon because her father doesn't care for the company she's keeping."

"Interesting."

"The man really hates me. Some people take to me and some people don't, but he just couldn't stomach me. Thought I was the lowest of the low. It really grinds a person down, you know. All the pressure he was putting on Robin, and both of us being as broke as we were, I'll tell you, it reached the point where I couldn't get any writing done."

"That's terrible," Ehrengraf said, his face clouded with concern. "The poetry left you?"

"That's what happened. It just wouldn't come to me. I'd sit there all day staring at a blank sheet of paper, and finally I'd say the hell with it and fire up a joint or get into the wine, and there's another day down the old chute. And then finally I found that bottle of bourbon and the next thing I knew—" the poet managed a brave smile "—well, according to you, I'm innocent."

"Of course you are innocent, sir."

"I wish I was convinced of that, Mr. Ehrengraf. I don't even see how you can be convinced."

"Because you are a poet," the diminutive attorney said. "Because, further, you are a client of Martin H. Ehrengraf. My clients are always innocent. That is the Ehrengraf presumption. Indeed, my income depends upon the innocence of my clients."

"I don't follow you."

"It's simple enough. My fees, as we've said, are quite high. But I collect them only if my efforts are successful. If a client of mine goes to prison, Mr. Telliford, he pays me nothing. I'm not even reimbursed for my expenses."

"That's incredible," Telliford said. "I never heard of anything like that. Do many lawyers work that way?"

"I believe I'm the only one. It's a pity more don't take up the custom. Other professionals as well, for that matter. Consider how much higher the percentage of successful operations might be if surgeons were paid on the basis of their results."

"Isn't that the truth. Hey, you know what's ironic?"

"What?"

"Mr. Littlefield. Robin's father. He could pay you that eighty thousand out of petty cash and never miss it. That's the kind of money he's got. But the way he feels about me, he'd pay to *send* me to prison, not to keep me out of it. In other words, if you worked for him you'd only get paid if you lost your case. Don't you think that's ironic?"

"Yes," said Ehrengraf. "I do indeed."

THE EHRENGRAF Obligation

When William Telliford stepped into Ehrengraf's office, the lawyer scarcely recognized him. The poet's beard was gone and his hair had received the attention of a fashionable barber. His jacket was black velvet, his trousers a cream-colored flannel. He was wearing a raw silk shirt and a bold paisley ascot.

He smiled broadly at Ehrengraf's reaction. "I guess I look different," he said.

"Different," Ehrengraf agreed.

"Well, I don't have to live like a slob now." The young man sat down in one of Ehrengraf's chairs, shot his cuff, and checked the time on an oversized gold watch. "Robin'll be coming by for me in half an hour," he said, "but I wanted to take the time to let you know how much I appreciated what you tried to do for me. You believed in my innocence when I didn't even have that much faith in myself. And I'm sure you would have been terrific in the courtroom if it had come to that."

"Fortunately it didn't."

"Right, but whoever would have guessed how it would turn out? Imagine old Jasper Littlefield killing Jan to frame me and get me out of his daughter's life. That's really a tough one to swallow. But he came over looking for Robin, and he found me drunk, and then it was evidently just a matter of taking the fire axe out of the case and taking me along with him to Jan's place and killing her and smearing her blood all over me. I must have been in worse than a blackout when it happened. I must have been passed out cold for him to be sure I wouldn't remember any of it."

"So it would seem."

"The police never did find the fire axe, and I wondered about that at the time. What I'd done with it, I mean, because deep down inside I really figured I must have been guilty. But what happened was Mr. Littlefield took the axe along with him, and then when he went crazy it was there for him to use."

"And use it he did."

"He sure did," Telliford said. "According to some psychologist they interviewed for one of the papers, he must have been repressing his basic instincts all his life. When he killed Jan for the purpose of framing me, it set something off inside him, some undercurrent of violence he'd been smothering for years and years. And then finally he up and dug out the fire axe, and he did a job on his wife and his son, chopped them both to hell and gone, and then he made a phone call to the police and confessed what he'd done and told about murdering Jan at the same time."

"Considerate of him," said Ehrengraf, "to make that phone call."

"I'll have to give him that," the poet said. "And then, before the cops could get there and pick him up, he took the fire axe and chopped through the veins in his wrists and bled to death."

"And you're a free man."

"And glad of it," Telliford said. "I'll tell you, it looks to me as though I'm sitting on top of the world. Robin's crazy about me and I'm all she's got in the world, me and the millions of bucks her father left her. With the rest of the family dead, she inherits every penny. No more slinging hash. No more starving in a garret. No more dressing like a slob. You like my new wardrobe?"

"It's quite a change," Ehrengraf said.

"Well, I realize now that I was getting sick of the way I looked, the life I was leading. Now I can live the way I want. I've got the freedom to do as I please with my life."

"That's wonderful."

"And you're the man who believed in me when nobody else did, myself included." Telliford smiled with genuine warmth. "I can't tell you how grateful I am. I was talking with Robin, and I had the idea that we ought to pay you your fee. You didn't actually get me off, of course, but your system is that you get paid no matter how your client gets off, just so he doesn't wind up in jail. That's how you explained it, isn't it?"

"That's right."

"That's what I said to Robin. But she said we didn't have any agreement to pay you eighty thousand dollars, as a matter of fact we didn't have any agreement to pay you anything, because you volunteered your services. In fact I would have gotten off the same way with my court-appointed attorney. I said that wasn't the point, but Robin said after all it's her money and she didn't see the point of giving you an eighty-thousand-dollar handout, that you were obviously well off and didn't need charity."

"Her father's daughter, I'd say."

"Huh? Anyway, it's her money and her decision to make, but I got her to agree that we'd pay for any expenses you had. So if you can come up with a figure—"

Ehrengraf shook his head. "You don't owe me a cent," he insisted. "I took your case out of a sense of obligation. And your lady friend is quite correct—I am not a charity case. Furthermore, my expenses on your behalf were extremely low, and in any case I should be more than happy to stand the cost myself."

"Well, if you're absolutely certain—"

"Quite certain, thank you." Ehrengraf smiled. "I'm most satisfied with the outcome of the case. Of course I regret the loss of Miss Littlefield's mother and brother, but at least there's a happy ending to it all. You're out of prison, you have no worries about money, your future is assured, and you can return to the serious business of writing poetry."

"Yeah," Telliford said.

"Is something wrong?"

"Not really. Just what you said about poetry. I suppose I'll get back to it sooner or later."

"Don't tell me your muse has deserted you?"

"Oh, I don't know," the young man said nervously. "It's just that, oh, I don't really seem to care much about poetry now, you know what I mean?"

"I'm not sure that I do."

"Well, I've got everything I want, you know? I've got the money to go all over the world and try all the things I've always wanted to try, and, oh, poetry just doesn't seem very important anymore." He laughed. "I remember what a kick I used to get when I'd check the mailbox and some little magazine would send me a check for one of my poems. Now what I usually got was fifty cents a line for poems, and that's from the magazines that paid anything, and most of them just gave you copies of the issue with the poem in it and that was that. That sonnet you liked, 'On a Train Through Kansas,' the magazine that took it paid me twenty-five cents a line. So I made three dollars and fifty cents for that poem, and by the time I submitted it here and there and everywhere, hell, my postage came to pretty nearly as much as I got for it."

"It's a scandal."

"But the thing is, when I didn't have any money, even a little check helped. Now, though, it's hard to take the whole thing seriously. But besides that, I just don't get poetic ideas anymore. And I just don't feel it." He forced a smile. "It's funny. Getting away from poetry hasn't been bothering me, but now that I'm talking with you about it I find myself feeling bad. As though by giving up poetry I'm letting you down or something."

"You're not letting me down," Ehrengraf said. "But to dismiss the talent you have, to let it languish—"

"Well, I just don't know if I've got it anymore," Telliford said. "That's the whole thing. I sit down and try to write a poem and it's just not there, you know what I mean? And Robin says why waste my time, that nobody really cares about poetry nowadays anyway, and I figure maybe she's right."

"Her father's daughter."

"Huh? Well, I'll tell you something that's ironic, anyway. I was having trouble writing poetry before I went to jail, what with the hassles from Robin's old man and all our problems and getting into the wine and the grass too much. And I'm having more troubles now, now that we've got plenty of money and Robin's father's out of our hair. But you know when I was really having no trouble at all?"

"When?"

"During the time I was in jail. There I was, stuck in that rotten cell with a lifetime in the penitentiary staring me in the face, and I swear I was averaging a poem every day. My mind was just clicking along. And I was writing good stuff, too." The young man drew an alligator billfold from the breast pocket of the velvet jacket, removed and unfolded a sheet of paper. “You liked the Kansas poem,” he said, “so why don’t you see what you think of this one?”

Ehrengraf read the poem. It seemed to be about birds, and included the line “Puppets dance from bloody strings.” Ehrengraf wasn’t sure what the poem meant but he knew he liked the sound of that line.

“It’s very good,” he said.

“Yeah, I thought you’d like it. And I wrote it in the jug, just wrote the words down like they were flowing out of a faucet, and now all I can write is checks. It’s ironic, isn’t it?”

“It certainly is,” said Ehrengraf.

It was a little over two weeks later when Ehrengraf met yet again with William Telliford. Once again, the meeting took place in the jail cell where the two had first made one another’s acquaintance.

“Mr. Ehrengraf,” the young man said. “Gee, I didn’t know if you would show up. I figured you’d wash your hands of me.”

“Why should I do that, sir?”

“Because they say I killed Robin. But I swear I didn’t do it!”

“Of course you didn’t.”

“I could have killed Jan, for all I knew. Because I was unconscious at the time, or in a blackout, or whatever it was. So I didn’t know what happened. But I was away from the apartment when Robin was killed, and I was awake. I hadn’t even been drinking much.”

“We’ll simply prove where you were.”

Telliford shook his head. “What we can’t prove is that Robin was alive when I left the apartment. I know she was, but how are we going to prove it?”

“We’ll find a way,” Ehrengraf said soothingly. “We know you’re innocent, don’t we?”

“Right.”

“Then there is nothing to worry about. Someone else must have gone to your house, taking that fire axe along for the express purpose of framing you for murder. Someone jealous of your success, perhaps. Someone who begrudged you your happiness."

"But who?"

"Leave that to me, sir. It's my job."

"Your job," Telliford said. "Well, this time you'll get well paid for your job, Mr. Ehrengraf. And your system is perfect for my case, let me tell you."

"How do you mean?"

"If I'm found innocent, I'll inherit all the money Robin inherited from her father. She made me her beneficiary. So I'll be able to pay you whatever you ask, eighty thousand dollars or even more."

"Eighty thousand will be satisfactory."

"And I'll pay it with pleasure. But if I'm found guilty, well, I won't get a dime."

"Because one cannot legally profit from a crime."

"Right. So if take the case on your usual terms—"

"I work on no other terms," Ehrengraf said. "And I would trust no one else with your case." He took a deep breath and held it in his lungs for a moment before continuing. "Mr. Telliford," he said, "your case is going to be a difficult one. You must appreciate that."

"I do."

"I shall of course do everything in my power on your behalf, acting always in your best interest. But you must recognize that the possibility exists that you will be convicted."

"And for a crime I didn't commit."

"Such miscarriages of justice do occasionally come to pass. It's tragic, I agree, but don't despair. Even if you're convicted, the appeal process is an exhaustive one. We can appeal your case again and again. You may have to serve some time in prison, Mr. Telliford, but there's always hope. And surely you know what Lovelace had to say on the subject."

"Lovelace?"

"Richard Lovelace. Born 1618, died 1657. 'To Althea, from Prison,' Mr. Telliford.

"Stone walls do not a prison make,
Nor iron bars a cage;
Minds innocent and quiet take
That for an hermitage.
If I have freedom in my love,
And in my soul am free,
Angels alone, that soar above,
Enjoy such liberty."

Telliford shuddered.

"'Stone walls and iron bars,'" he said.

"Have faith, sir."

"I'll try."

"At least you have your poetry. Are you sufficiently supplied with paper and pencil? I'll make sure your needs are seen to."

"Maybe it would help me to write some poetry. Maybe it would take my mind off things."

"Perhaps it would. And I'll devote myself wholeheartedly to your defense, sir, whether I ever see a penny for my troubles or not." He drew himself up to his full height. "After all," he said, "it's my obligation. 'I could not love thee, dear, so much, Loved I not Honour more.' That's also Lovelace, Mr. Telliford. 'To Lucasta, Going to the Wars.' Good day, Mr. Telliford. You have nothing to worry about."

The EHRENGRAF Alternative

"Things are seldom what they seem,
Skim milk masquerades as cream."
—William Schwenk Gilbert

"What's most unfortunate," Ehrengraf said, "is that there seems to be a witness."

Evelyn Throop nodded in fervent agreement. "Mrs. Keppner," she said. "Howard Bierstadt's housekeeper."

"She was devoted to him. She'd been with him for years."

"And she claims she saw you shoot him three times in the chest."

"I know," Evelyn Throop said. "I can't imagine why she would say something like that. It's completely untrue."

A thin smile turned up the corners of Martin Ehrengraf's mouth. Already he felt himself warming to his client, exhilarated by the prospect of acting in her defense. It was the little lawyer's great good fortune always to find himself representing innocent clients, but few of those clients were as single-minded as Miss Throop in proclaiming their innocence.

The woman sat on the edge of her iron cot with her shapely legs crossed at the ankle. She seemed so utterly in possession of herself that she might have been almost anywhere but in a jail cell, charged with the murder of her lover. Her age, according to the papers, was forty-six. Ehrengraf would have guessed her to be perhaps a dozen years younger. She was not rich—Ehrengraf, like most lawyers, did have a special fondness for wealthy clients—but she had excellent breeding. It was evident not only in her exquisite facial bones but in her positively ducal self-assurance.

"I'm sure we'll uncover the explanation of Mrs. Keppner's calumny," he said gently. "For now, why don't we go over what actually happened."

"Certainly. I was at my home that evening when Howard called. He was in a mood and wanted to see me. I drove over to his house. He made drinks for both of us and paced around a great deal. He was extremely agitated."

"Over what?"

"Leona wanted him to marry her. Leona Weybright."

"The cookbook writer?"

"Yes. Howard was not the sort of man to get married, or even to limit himself to a single relationship. He believed in a double standard and was quite open about it. He expected his women to be faithful while reserving the option of infidelity to himself. If one was going to be involved with Howard Bierstadt, one had to accept this."

"As you accepted it."

"I accepted it," Evelyn Throop agreed. "Leona evidently pretended to accept it but could not, and Howard didn't know what to do about her. He wanted to break up with her but was afraid of the possible consequences. He thought she might turn suicidal and he didn't want her death on his conscience."

"And he discussed all of this with you."

"Oh, yes. He often confided in me about his relationship with Leona." Evelyn Throop permitted herself a smile. "I played a very important role in his life, Mr. Ehrengraf. I suppose he would have married me if there'd been any reason to do so. I was his true confidante. Leona was just one of a long string of mistresses."

Ehrengraf nodded. "According to the prosecution," he said carefully, "you were pressuring him to marry you."

"That's quite untrue."

"No doubt." He smiled. "Continue."

The woman sighed. "There's not much more to say. He went into the other room to freshen our drinks. There was the report of a gunshot."

"I believe there were three shots."

"Perhaps there were. I can remember only the volume of the noise. It was so startling. I rushed in immediately and saw him on the floor, the gun by his outstretched hand. I guess I bent over and picked up the gun. I don't remember doing so, but I must have done because the next thing I knew I was standing there holding the gun." Evelyn Throop closed her eyes, evidently overwhelmed by the memory. "Then Mrs. Keppner was there—I believe she screamed, and then she went off to call the police. I just stood there for a while and then I guess I sat down in a chair and waited for the police to come and tell me what to do."

"And they brought you here and put you in a cell."

"Yes. I was quite astonished. I couldn't imagine why they would do such a thing, and then it developed that Mrs. Keppner had sworn she saw me shoot Howard."

Ehrengraf was respectfully silent for a moment. Then he said, "It seems they found some corroboration for Mrs. Keppner's story."

"What do you mean?"

"The gun," Ehrengraf said. "A revolver. I believe it was registered to you, was it not?"

"It was my gun."

"How did Mr. Bierstadt happen to have it?"

"I brought it to him."

"At his request?"

"Yes. When we spoke on the telephone, he specifically asked me to bring the gun. He said something about wanting to protect himself from burglars. I never thought he would shoot himself."

"But he did."

"He must have done. He was upset about Leona. Perhaps he felt guilty, or that there was no way to avoid hurting her."

"Wasn't there a test?" Ehrengraf mused. "As I recall, there were no nitrite particles found in Mr. Bierstadt's hand, which would seem to indicate he had not fired a gun recently."

"I don't really understand those tests," Evelyn Throop said. "But I'm told they're not absolutely conclusive."

"And the police gave you a test as well," Ehrengraf went on. "Didn't they?"

"Yes."

"And found nitrite particles in your right hand."

"Of course," Evelyn Throop said. "I'd fired the gun that evening before I took it along to Howard's house. I hadn't used it in the longest time, since I first practiced with it at a pistol range, so I cleaned it, and to make sure it was in good operating condition I test-fired it before I went to Howard's."

"At a pistol range?"

"That wouldn't have been convenient. I just stopped at a deserted spot along a country road and fired a few shots."

"I see."

"I told the police all of this, of course."

"Of course. Before they gave you the paraffin test?"

"After the test, as it happens. The incident had quite slipped my mind in the excitement of the moment, but they gave me the test and said it was evident I'd fired a gun, and at that point I recalled having stopped the car and firing off a couple of rounds before continuing on to Howard's."

"Where you gave Mr. Bierstadt the gun."

"Yes."

"Whereupon he in due course took it off into another room and fired three shots into his heart," Ehrengraf murmured. "Your Mr. Bierstadt would look to be one of the most determined suicides in human memory."

"You don't believe me."

"But I do believe you," he said. "Which is to say that I believe you did not shoot Mr. Bierstadt. Whether or not he did in fact die by his own hand is not, of course, something to which either you or I can testify."

"How else could he have died?" The woman's gaze narrowed. "Unless he really was genuinely afraid of burglars, and unless he did surprise one in the other room. But wouldn't I have heard sounds of a struggle? Of course, I was in another room a fair distance away, and there was music playing, and I did have things on my mind."

"I'm sure you did."

"And perhaps Mrs. Keppner saw the burglar shoot Howard, and then she fainted or something. I suppose that's possible, isn't it?"

"Eminently possible," Ehrengraf assured her.

"She might have come to when I had already entered the room and picked up the gun, and the whole incident could have been compressed in her mind. She wouldn't remember having fainted and so she might now actually believe she saw me kill Howard, while all along she saw something entirely different."

Evelyn Throop had been looking off into the middle distance as she formulated her theory, and now she focused her eyes upon the diminutive attorney. "It could have happened that way," she said, "couldn't it?"

"It could have happened precisely that way," Ehrengraf said. "It could have happened in any of innumerable ways. Ah, Miss Throop—" now the lawyer rubbed his small hands together "—that's the whole beauty of it. There are any number of alternatives to the prosecution's argument, but of course they don't see them. Give the police a supposedly ironclad case and they look no further. It is not their task to examine alternatives. But it is our task, Miss Throop, to find not merely an alternative but the correct alternative, the ideal alternative. And in just that fashion we will make a free woman of you."

"You seem very confident, Mr. Ehrengraf."

"I am."

"And prepared to believe in my innocence."

"Unequivocally. Without question."

"I find that refreshing," Evelyn Throop said. "I even believe you'll get me acquitted."

"I fully expect to," Ehrengraf said. "Now let me see, is there anything else we have to discuss at present?"

"Yes."

"And what would that be?"

"Your fee," said Evelyn Throop.

Back in his office, seated behind a desk which he kept as untidy as he kept his own person immaculate, Martin H. Ehrengraf sat back and contemplated the many extraordinary qualities of his latest client. In his considerable experience, while clients were not invariably opposed to a discussion of his fees, they were certainly loath to raise the matter. But Evelyn Throop, possessor of dove-gray eyes and remarkable facial bones, had proved an exception.

"My fees are high," Ehrengraf had told her, "but they are payable only in the event that my clients are acquitted. If you don't emerge from this ordeal scot-free, you owe me nothing. Even my expenses will be at my expense."

"And if I get off?"

"Then you will owe me one hundred thousand dollars. And I must emphasize, Miss Throop, that the fee will be due me however you win your freedom. It is not inconceivable that neither of us will ever see the inside of a courtroom, that your release when it comes will appear not to have been the result of my efforts at all. I will, nevertheless, expect to be paid in full."

The gray eyes looked searchingly into the lawyer's own. "Yes," she said after a moment. "Yes, of course. Well, that seems fair. If I'm released I won't really care how the end was accomplished, will I?"

Ehrengraf said nothing. Clients often whistled a different tune at a later date, but one could burn that bridge when one came to it.

"One hundred thousand dollars seems reasonable," the woman continued. "I suppose any sum would seem reasonable when one's life and liberty hang in the balance. Of course, you must know I have no money of my own."

"Perhaps your family—"

She shook her head. "I can trace my ancestors back to William the Conqueror," she said, "and there were Throops who made their fortune in whaling and the China trade, but I'm afraid the money's run out over the generations. However, I shouldn't have any problem paying your fee."

"Oh?"

"I'm Howard's chief beneficiary," she explained. "I've seen his will and it makes it unmistakably clear that I held first place in his affections. After a small cash bequest to Mrs. Keppner for her loyal years of service, and after leaving his art collection—which, I grant you, is substantial—to Leona, the remainder comes to me. There may be a couple of cash bequests to charities but nothing that amounts to much. So while I'll have to wait for the will to make its way through probate, I'm sure I can borrow on my expectations and pay you your fee within a matter of days of my release from jail, Mr. Ehrengraf."

"A day that should come in short order," Ehrengraf said.

"That's your department," Evelyn Throop said, and smiled serenely.

Ehrengraf smiled now, recalling her smile, and made a little tent of his fingertips on the desk top. An exceptional woman, he told himself, and one on whose behalf it would be an honor to extend himself. It was difficult, of course. Shot with the woman's own gun, and a witness to swear that she'd shot him. Difficult, certainly, but scarcely impossible.

The little lawyer leaned back, closed his eyes, and considered alternatives.

Some days later, Ehrengraf was seated at his desk reading the poems of William Ernest Henley, who had written so confidently of being the master of one's fate and the captain of one's soul. The telephone rang. Ehrengraf set his book down, located the instrument amid the desk top clutter, and answered it.

"Ehrengraf," said Ehrengraf.

He listened for a moment, spoke briefly in reply, and replaced the receiver.

Smiling brightly, he started for the door, then paused to check his appearance in a mirror.

His tie was navy blue, with a demure below-the-knot pattern of embroidered rams' heads. For a moment Ehrengraf thought of stopping at his house and changing it for his Caedmon Society necktie, one he'd taken to wearing on triumphal occasions. He glanced at his watch and decided not to squander the time.

Later, recalling the decision, he wondered if it hinted at prescience.

"Quite remarkable," Evelyn Throop said. "Although I suppose I should have at least considered the possibility that Mrs. Keppner was lying. After all, I knew for a fact that she was testifying to something that didn't happen to be true. But for some reason I assumed it was an honest mistake on her part."

"One hesitates to believe the worst of people," Ehrengraf said.

"That's exactly it, of course. Besides, I rather took her for granted."

"So, it appears, did Mr. Bierstadt."

"And that was his mistake, wasn't it?" Evelyn Throop sighed. "Dora Keppner had been with him for years. Who would have guessed she'd been in love with him? Although I gather their relationship was physical at one point."

"There was a suggestion to that effect in the note she left."

"And I understand he wanted to get rid of her—to discharge her."

"The note seems to have indicated considerable mental disturbance," Ehrengraf said. "There were other jottings in a notebook found in Mrs. Keppner's attic bedroom. The impression seems to be that either she and her employer had been intimate in the past or that she entertained a fantasy to that effect. Her attitude in recent weeks apparently became less and less the sort proper to a servant, and either Mr. Bierstadt intended to let her go or she feared that he did and—well, we know what happened."

"She shot him." Evelyn Throop frowned. "She must have been in the room when he went to freshen the drinks. I thought he'd put the gun in his pocket but perhaps he still had it in his hand. He would have set it down when he made the drinks and she could have snatched it up and shot him and been out of the room before I got there." The gray eyes moved to encounter Ehrengraf's. "She didn't leave any fingerprints on the gun."

"She seems to have worn gloves. She was wearing a pair when she took her own life. A test indicated nitrite particles in the right glove."

"Couldn't they have gotten there when she committed suicide?"

"It's unlikely," Ehrengraf said. "She didn't shoot herself, you see. She took poison."

"How awful," Evelyn Throop said. "I hope it was quick."

"Mercifully so," said Ehrengraf. Clearly this woman was the captain of her soul, he thought, not to mention master of her fate. Or ought it to be mistress of her fate? And yet, he realized abruptly, she was not entirely at ease.

"I've been released," she said, "as is of course quite obvious. All charges have been dropped. A man from the District Attorney's Office explained everything to me."

"That was considerate of him."

"He didn't seem altogether happy. I had the feeling he didn't really believe I was innocent after all."

"People believe what they wish to believe," Ehrengraf said smoothly. "The state's whole case collapses without their star witness, and after that witness has confessed to the crime herself and taken her life in the bargain, well, what does it matter what a stubborn district attorney chooses to believe?"

"I'm sure you're right."

"The important thing is that you've been set free. You're innocent of all charges."

"Yes."

His eyes searched hers. "Is there a problem, Miss Throop?"

"There is, Mr. Ehrengraf."

"Dear lady," he began, "if you could just tell me—"

"The problem concerns your fee."

Ehrengraf's heart sank. Why did so many clients disappoint him in precisely this fashion? At the onset, with the sword of justice hanging over their throats, they agreed eagerly to whatever he proposed. Remove the sword and their agreeability went with it.

But that was not it at all.

"The most extraordinary thing," Evelyn Throop was saying. "I told you the terms of Howard's will. The paintings to Leona, a few thousand dollars here and there to various charities, a modest bequest to Mrs. Keppner—I suppose she won't get that now, will she?"

"Hardly."

"Well, that's something. Though it doesn't amount to much. At any rate, the balance is to go to me. The residue, after the bequests have been made and all debts settled and the state and federal taxes been paid, all that remains comes to me."

"So you explained."

"I intended to pay you out of what I received, Mr. Ehrengraf. Well, you're more than welcome to every cent I get. You can buy yourself a couple of hamburgers and a milkshake."

"I don't understand."

"It's the damned paintings," Evelyn Throop said. "They're worth an absolute fortune. I didn't realize how much he spent on them in the first place or how rapidly they appreciated in value. Nor did I have any idea how deeply mortgaged everything else he owned was. He had some investment reversals over the past few months and he'd taken out a second mortgage on his home and sold off stocks and other holdings. There's a little cash and a certain amount of equity in the real estate, but it'll take all of that to pay the estate taxes on the several million dollars' worth of paintings that go free and clear to that bitch Leona."

"You have to pay the taxes?"

"No question about it," she said bitterly. "The estate pays the taxes and settles the debts. Then all the paintings go straight to America's favorite cook. I hope she chokes on them." Evelyn Throop sighed heavily, collected herself. "Please forgive the dramatics, Mr. Ehrengraf."

"They're quite understandable, dear lady."

"I didn't intend to lose control of myself in that fashion. But I feel this deeply. I know Howard had no intention of disinheriting me and having that woman get everything. It was his unmistakable intention to leave me the greater portion, and a cruel trick of fate has thwarted him in that purpose. Mr. Ehrengraf, I owe you one hundred thousand dollars. That was our agreement and I consider myself bound by it."

Ehrengraf made no reply.

"But I don't know how I can possibly pay you. Oh, I'll pay what I can, as I can, but I'm a woman of modest means. I couldn't honestly expect to discharge the debt in full within my lifetime."

"My dear Miss Throop." Ehrengraf was moved, and his hand went involuntarily to the knot of his necktie. "My dear Miss Throop," he said again, "I beg you not to worry yourself. Do you know Henley, Miss Throop?"

"Henley?"

"The poet," said Ehrengraf, and quoted:

> "In the fell clutch of circumstance,
> I have not winced nor cried aloud:
> Under the bludgeonings of chance
> My head is bloody, but unbowed.

"William Ernest Henley, Miss Throop. Born 1849, died 1903. Bloody but unbowed, Miss Throop. 'I have not yet begun to fight.' That was John Paul Jones, Miss Throop, not a poet at all, a naval commander of the Revolutionary War, but the sentiment, dear lady, is worthy of a poet. 'Things are seldom what they seem, Skim milk masquerades as cream.' William Schwenk Gilbert, Miss Throop."

"I don't understand."

"Alternatives, Miss Throop. Alternatives!" The little lawyer was on his feet, pacing, gesticulating with precision. "I tell you only what I told you before. There are always alternatives available to us."

The gray eyes narrowed in thought. "I suppose you mean we could sue to overturn the will," she said. "That occurred to me, but I thought you only handled criminal cases."

"And so I do."

"I wonder if I could find another who would contest the will on a contingency basis. Perhaps you know someone—"

"Ah, Miss Throop," said Ehrengraf, sitting back down and placing his fingertips together. "Contest the will? Life is too short for litigation. An unlikely sentiment for an attorney to voice, I know, but nonetheless valid for it. Put lawsuits far from your mind. Let us first see if we cannot find—" a smile blossomed on his lips "—the Ehrengraf alternative."

Ehrengraf, a shine on his black wing-tip shoes and a white carnation on his lapel, strode briskly up the cinder path from his car to the center entrance of the Bierstadt house. In the crisp autumn air, the ivy-covered brick mansion in its spacious grounds took on an aura suggestive of a college campus. Ehrengraf noticed this and touched his tie, a distinctive specimen sporting a half-inch stripe of royal blue flanked by two narrower stripes, one of gold and the other of a particularly vivid green, all on a deep navy field. It was the tie he had very nearly worn to the meeting with his client some weeks earlier.

Now, he trusted, it would be rather more appropriate. He eschewed the doorbell in favor of the heavy brass knocker, and in a matter of seconds the door swung inward. Evelyn Throop met him with a smile. "Dear Mr. Ehrengraf," she said. "It's kind of you to meet me here. In poor Howard's home."

"Your home now," Ehrengraf murmured.

"Mine," she agreed. "Of course, there are legal processes to be gone through, but I've been allowed to take possession. And I think I'm going to be able to keep the place. Now that the paintings are mine, I'll be able to sell some of them to pay the taxes and settle other claims against the estate. But let me show you around. This is the living room, of course, and here's the room where Howard and I were having drinks that night—"

"That fateful night," said Ehrengraf.

"And here's the room where Howard was killed. He was preparing drinks at the sideboard over there. He was lying here when I found him. And—" Ehrengraf watched politely as his client pointed out where everything had taken place. Then he followed her to another room where he accepted a small glass of Calvados.

For herself, Evelyn Throop poured a pony of Bénédictine.

"What shall we drink to?" she asked him.

To your spectacular eyes, he thought, but suggested instead that she propose a toast.

"To the Ehrengraf alternative," she said.

They drank.

"The Ehrengraf alternative," she said again. "I didn't know what to expect when we last saw each other. I thought you must have had some sort of complicated legal maneuver in mind, perhaps some way around the extortionate tax burden the government levies upon even the most modest inheritance. I had no idea the whole circumstances of poor Howard's murder would wind up turned utterly upside down."

"It was quite extraordinary," Ehrengraf allowed.

"I had been astonished enough to learn that Mrs. Keppner had murdered Howard and then taken her own life. Imagine how I felt to learn that she wasn't a murderer and that she hadn't committed suicide but that she'd actually herself been murdered."

"Life keeps surprising us," Ehrengraf said.

"And Leona Weybright winds up hoist on her own soufflé. The funny thing is that I was right in the first place. Howard was afraid of Leona, and evidently he had every reason to be. He'd apparently written her a note, insisting that they stop seeing each other."

Ehrengraf nodded. "The police found the note when they searched her quarters. Of course, she insisted she had never seen it before."

"What else could she say?" Evelyn Throop took another delicate sip of Bénédictine, and Ehrengraf's heart thrilled at the sight of her pink tongue against the brim of the tiny glass. "But I don't see how she can expect anyone to believe her. She murdered Howard, didn't she?"

"It would be hard to establish that beyond a reasonable doubt," Ehrengraf said. "The supposition exists. However, Miss Weybright does have an alibi, and it might not be easily shaken. And the only witness to the murder, Mrs. Keppner, is no longer available to give testimony."

"Because Leona killed her."

Ehrengraf nodded. "And that," he said, "very likely can be established."

"Because Mrs. Keppner's suicide note was a forgery."

"So it would appear," Ehrengraf said. "An artful forgery, but a forgery nevertheless. And the police seem to have found earlier drafts of that very note in Miss Weybright's desk. One was typed on the very machine at which she prepares her cookbook manuscripts. Others were written with a pen found in her desk, and the ink matched that on the note Mrs.

Keppner purportedly left behind. Some of the drafts are in an imitation of the dead woman's handwriting, one in a sort of mongrel cross between the two women's penmanship, and one—evidently she was just trying to get the wording to her liking—was in Miss Weybright's own unmistakable hand. Circumstantial evidence, all of it, but highly suggestive."

"And there was other evidence, wasn't there?"

"Indeed there was. When Mrs. Keppner's body was found, there was a glass on a nearby table, a glass with a residue of water in it. An analysis of the water indicated the presence of a deadly poison, and an autopsy indicated that Mrs. Keppner's death had been caused ingesting that very substance. The police, combining two and two, concluded not illogically that Mrs. Keppner had drunk a glass of water with the poison in it."

"But that's not how it happened?"

"Apparently not. Because the autopsy also indicated that the deceased had had a piece of cake not long before she died."

"And the cake was poisoned?"

"I should think it must have been," Ehrengraf said carefully, "because police investigators happened to find a cake with one wedge missing, wrapped securely in aluminum foil and tucked away in Miss Weybright's freezer. And that cake, when thawed and subjected to chemical analysis, proved to have been laced with the very poison which caused the death of poor Mrs. Keppner."

Miss Throop looked thoughtful. "How did Leona try to get out of that?"

"She denied she ever saw the cake before and insisted she had never baked it."

"And?"

"And it seems to have been prepared precisely according to an original recipe in her present cookbook-in-progress."

"I suppose the book will never be published now."

"On the contrary, I believe the publisher has tripled the initial print order." Ehrengraf drew a breath. "As I understand it, the presumption is that Miss Weybright was desperate at the prospect of losing the unfortunate Mr. Bierstadt. She wanted him, and if she couldn't have him alive she wanted him dead. But she didn't want to be punished for his murder, nor did she want to lose out on whatever she stood to gain from his will. By framing you for his murder, she thought she could increase the portion due her. Actually, the language of the will probably would not have facilitated this, but she evidently didn't realize it, any more than she realized that by receiving the paintings she would have the lion's share of the estate. In any event, she must have been obsessed with the idea of killing her lover and seeing her rival pay for the crime."

"How did Mrs. Keppner get into the act?"

"We may never know for certain. Was the housekeeper in on the plot all along? Did she actually fire the fatal shots and then turn into a false witness? Or did Miss Weybright commit the murder and leave Mrs. Keppner to testify against you? Or did Mrs. Keppner see what she oughtn't to have seen and then, after lying about you, try her hand at blackmailing Miss Weybright? Whatever the actual circumstances, Miss Weybright realized that Mrs. Keppner represented either an immediate or a potential hazard."

"And so Leona killed her."

"And had no trouble doing so." One might call it a piece of cake, Ehrengraf forbore to say. "At that point it became worth her while to let Mrs. Keppner play the role of murderess. Perhaps Miss Weybright became acquainted with the nature of the will and the estate itself and realized that she would already be in line to receive the greater portion of the estate, that it was not necessary to frame you. Furthermore, she saw that you were not about to plead to a reduced charge or to attempt a Frankie-and-Johnny defense, as it were. By shunting the blame onto a dead Mrs. Keppner, she forestalled the possibility of a detailed investigation which might have pointed the finger of guilt in her own direction."

"My goodness," Evelyn Throop said. "It's quite extraordinary, isn't it?"

"It is," Ehrengraf agreed.

"And Leona will stand trial?"

"For Mrs. Keppner's murder."

"Will she be convicted?"

"One never knows what a jury will do," Ehrengraf said. "That's one reason I much prefer to spare my own clients the indignity of a trial."

He thought for a moment. "The district attorney might or might not have enough evidence to secure a conviction. Of course, more evidence might come to light between now and the trial. For that matter, evidence in Miss Weybright's favor might turn up."

"If she has the right lawyer."

"An attorney can often make a difference," Ehrengraf allowed. "But I'm afraid the man Miss Weybright has engaged won't do her much good. I suspect she'll wind up convicted of first-degree manslaughter or something of the sort. A few years in confined quarters and she'll have been rehabilitated. Perhaps she'll emerge from the experience with a slew of new recipes."

"Poor Leona," Evelyn Throop said, and shuddered delicately.

"Ah, well," Ehrengraf said. "'Life is bitter,' as our Mr. Henley reminds us in a poem. He goes on to say:

> "Riches won but mock the old, unable years;
> Fame's a pearl that hides beneath a sea of tears;
> Love must wither, or must live alone and weep.
> In the sunshine, through the leaves, across the flowers,
> While we slumber, death approaches through the hours...
> Let me sleep.

"Riches, fame, love—and yet we seek them, do we not? That will be one hundred thousand dollars, Miss Throop, and—ah, you have the check all drawn, have you?" He accepted it from her, folded it, and tucked it into a pocket.

"It is rare," he said, "to meet a woman so businesslike and yet so unequivocally feminine. And so attractive."

There was a small silence. Then: "Mr. Ehrengraf? Would you care to see the rest of the house?"

"I'd like that," said Ehrengraf, and smiled his little smile.

The EHRENGRAF Nostrum

"In the world's broad field of battle,
In the bivouac of Life,
Be not like dumb, driven cattle!
Be a hero in the strife!"
—Henry Wadsworth Longfellow

Gardner Bridgewater paced to and fro over Martin Ehrengraf's office carpet, reminding the little lawyer rather less of a caged jungle cat than—what? He doth bestride the narrow world like a Colossus, Ehrengraf thought, echoing Shakespeare's Cassius. But what, really, did a Colossus look like? Ehrengraf wasn't sure, but the alleged uxoricide was unquestionably colossal, and there he was, bestriding all over the place as if determined to wear holes in the rug.

"If I'd wanted to kill the woman," Bridgewater said, hitting one of his hands with the other, "I'd have damn well done it. By cracking her over the head with something heavy. A lamp base. A hammer. A fireplace poker."

An anvil, Ehrengraf thought. A stove. A Volkswagen.

"Or I might have wrung her neck," said Bridgewater, flexing his fingers. "Or I might have beaten her to death with my hands."

Ehrengraf thought of Longfellow's village blacksmith. "'The smith, a mighty man is he, with large and sinewy hands,'" he murmured.

"I beg your pardon?"

"Nothing important," said Ehrengraf. "You're saying, I gather, that if murderous impulses had overwhelmed you, you would have put them into effect in a more spontaneous and direct manner."

"Well, I certainly wouldn't have poisoned her. Poison's sneaky. It's the weapon of the weak, the devious, the cowardly."

"And yet your wife was poisoned."

"That's what they say. After dinner Wednesday she complained of headache and nausea. She took a couple of pills and lay down for a nap. She got up feeling worse, couldn't breathe. I rushed her to the hospital. Her heart ceased beating before I'd managed to fill out the questionnaire about medical insurance."

"And the cause of death," Ehrengraf said, "was a rather unusual poison."

Bridgewater nodded. "Cydonex," he said. "A tasteless, odorless, crystalline substance, a toxic hydrocarbon developed serendipitously as a by-product in the extrusion-molding of plastic dashboard figurines. Alyssa's system contained enough Cydonex to kill a person twice her size."

"You had recently purchased an eight-ounce canister of Cydonex."

"I had," Bridgewater said. "We had squirrels in the attic and I couldn't get rid of the wretched little beasts. The branches of several of our trees are within leaping distance of our roof and attic windows, and squirrels have quite infested the premises. They're noisy and filthy creatures, and clever at avoiding traps and poisoned baits. Isn't it extraordinary that a civilization with the capacity to devise napalm and Agent Orange can't come up with something for the control of rodents in a man's attic?"

"So you decided to exterminate them with Cydonex?"

"I thought it was worth a try. I mixed it into peanut butter and put gobs of it here and there in the attic. Squirrels are mad for peanut butter, especially the crunchy kind. They'll eat the creamy, but the crunchy really gets them."

"And yet you discarded the Cydonex. Investigators found the almost full canister near the bottom of the garbage can."

"I was worried about the possible effects. I recently saw a neighbor's dog with a squirrel in his jaws, and it struck me that a poisoned squirrel, reeling from the effects of the Cydonex, might be easy prey for a neighborhood pet, who would in turn be the poison's victim. Besides, as I said, poison's a sneak's weapon. Even a squirrel deserves a more direct approach."

A narrow smile blossomed for an instant on Ehrengraf's thin lips. Then it was gone. "One wonders," he said, "how the Cydonex got into your wife's system."

"It's a mystery to me, Mr. Ehrengraf. Unless poor Alyssa ate some peanut butter off the attic floor, I'm damned if I know where she got it."

"Of course," Ehrengraf said gently, "the police have their own theory."

"The police."

"Indeed. They seem to believe that you mixed a lethal dose of Cydonex into your wife's wine at dinner. The poison, tasteless and odorless as it is, would have been undetectable in plain water, let alone wine. What sort of wine was it, if I may ask?"

"Nuits-St.-Georges."

"And the main course?"

"Veal, I think. What difference does it make?"

"Nuits-St.-Georges would have overpowered the veal," Ehrengraf said thoughtfully. "No doubt it would have overpowered the Cydonex as well. The police said the wineglasses had been washed out, although the rest of the dinner dishes remained undone."

"The wineglasses are Waterford. I always do them up by hand, while Alyssa put everything else in the dishwasher."

"Indeed." Ehrengraf straightened up behind his desk, his hand fastening upon the knot of his tie. It was a small precise knot, and the tie itself was a two-inch-wide silk knit the approximate color of a bottle of Nuits-St.-Georges. The little lawyer wore a white-on-white shirt with French cuffs and a spread collar, and his suit was navy with a barely perceptible scarlet stripe. "As your lawyer," he said, "I must raise unpleasant points."

"Go right ahead."

"You have a mistress, a young woman who is expecting your child. You and your wife were not getting along. Your wife refused to give you a divorce. Your business, while extremely profitable, has been experiencing recent cash-flow problems. Your wife's life was insured in the amount of five hundred thousand dollars with yourself as beneficiary. In addition, you are her sole heir, and her estate after taxes will still be considerable. Is all of that correct?"

"It is," Bridgewater admitted. "The police found it significant."

"I'm not surprised."

Bridgewater leaned forward suddenly, placing his large and sinewy hands upon Ehrengraf's desk. He looked capable of yanking the top off it and dashing it against the wall. "Mr. Ehrengraf," he said, his voice barely above a whisper, "do you think I should plead guilty?"

"Of course not."

"I could plead to a reduced charge."

"But you're innocent," Ehrengraf said. "My clients are always innocent, Mr. Bridgewater. My fees are high, sir. One might even pronounce them towering. But I collect them only if I win an acquittal or if the charges against my client are peremptorily dismissed. I intend to demonstrate your innocence, Mr. Bridgewater, and my fee system provides me with the keenest incentive toward that end."

"I see."

"Now," said Ehrengraf, coming out from behind his desk and rubbing his small hands briskly together, "let us look at the possibilities. Your wife ate the same meal you did, is that correct?"

"It is."

"And drank the same wine?"

'Yes. The residue in the bottle was unpoisoned. But I could have put Cydonex directly into her glass."

"But you didn't, Mr. Bridgewater, so let us not weigh ourselves down with what you could have done. She became ill after the meal, I believe you said."

"Yes. She was headachy and nauseous."

"Headachy and nauseated, Mr. Bridgewater. That she was nauseous in the bargain would be a subjective conclusion of your own. She lay down for a nap?"

"Yes."

"But first she took something."

"Yes, that's right."

"Aspirin, something of that sort?"

"I suppose it's mostly aspirin," Bridgewater said. "It's a patent medicine called Darnitol. Alyssa took it for everything from cramps to athlete's foot."

"Darnitol," Ehrengraf said. "An analgesic?"

"An analgesic, an anodyne, an antispasmodic, a panacea, a catholicon, a cure-all, a nostrum. Alyssa believed in it, Mr. Ehrengraf, and my guess would be that her belief was responsible for much of the preparation's efficacy. I don't take pills, never have, and my headaches seemed to pass as quickly as hers." He laughed shortly. "In any event, Darnitol proved an inadequate antidote for Cydonex."

"Hmm," said Ehrengraf.

"To think it was the Darnitol that killed her."

Five weeks had passed since their initial meeting, and events in the interim had done a great deal to improve both the circumstances and the spirit of Ehrengraf's client. Gardner Bridgewater was no longer charged with his wife's murder.

"It was one of the first things I thought of," Ehrengraf said. "The police had their vision clouded by the extraordinary coincidence of your purchase and use of Cydonex as a vehicle for the extermination of squirrels. But my view was based on the presumption of your innocence, and I was able to discard this coincidence as irrelevant. It wasn't until other innocent men and women began to die of Cydonex poisoning that a pattern began to emerge. A schoolteacher in Kenmore. A retired steelworker in Lackawanna. A young mother in Orchard Park."

"And more," Bridgewater said. "Eleven in all, weren't there?"

"Twelve," Ehrengraf said. "But for diabolical cleverness on the part of the poisoner, he could never have gotten away with it for so long."

"I don't understand how he managed it."

"By leaving no incriminating residue," Ehrengraf explained. "We've had poisoners of this sort before, tainting tablets of some nostrum or other. And there was a man in Boston, I believe it was, who stirred arsenic into the sugar in coffee-shop dispensers. With any random mass murder of that sort, sooner or later a pattern emerges. But this killer only tampered with a single capsule in each bottle of Darnitol. The victim might consume capsules with impunity until the one fatal pill was swallowed, whereupon there would be no evidence remaining in the bottle, no telltale leftover capsule to give the police a clue."

"Good heavens."

"Indeed. The police did in fact test as a matter of course the bottles of Darnitol which were invariably found among the effects. But the pills invariably proved innocent. Finally, when the death toll mounted high enough, the fact that Darnitol was associated with every single death proved indismissable. The police seized drugstore stocks of the painkiller, and again and again bottles turned out to have a single tainted capsule in with the legitimate pills."

"And the actual killer—"

"Will be found, I shouldn't doubt, in the course of time." Ehrengraf straightened his tie, a stylish specimen showing a half-inch stripe of royal blue flanked by narrower stripes, one of gold and the other of a green, all displayed on a field of navy blue. The tie was that of the Caedmon Society, and it brought back memories. "Some disgruntled employee of the Darnitol manufacturer, I shouldn't wonder," said Ehrengraf carelessly. "That's usually the case in this sort of affair. Or some unbalanced chap who took the pill himself and was unhappy with the results. Twelve dead, plus your wife of course, and a company on the verge of ruin, because I shouldn't think too many people are rushing down to their local pharmacy and purchasing Extra-Strength Darnitol."

"There's a joke going round," Bridgewater said, flexing his large and sinewy hands. "Patient calls his doctor, says he's got a headache, an upset stomach, whatever. Doctor says, 'Take Darnitol and call me in the Hereafter.'"

"Indeed."

Bridgewater frowned. "I suppose," he said, "the real killer may never be found."

"Oh, I suspect he will," Ehrengraf said. "In the interests of rounding things out, you know. And, speaking of rounding things out, sir, if you've your checkbook with you—"

"Ah, yes," said Bridgewater. He made his check payable to Martin H. Ehrengraf and filled in the sum, which was a large one. He paused then, his pen hovering over the space for his signature. Perhaps he reflected for a moment on the curious business of paying so great an amount to a person who, on the face of it, had taken no concrete action on his behalf.

But who is to say what thoughts go through a man's mind? Bridgewater signed the check, tore it from the checkbook, and presented it with a flourish.

"What would you drink with veal?" he demanded.

"I beg your pardon?"

"You said the Nuits-St.-Georges would be overpowering with veal. What would you choose?"

"I shouldn't choose veal in the first place. I don't eat meat."

"Don't eat meat?" Bridgewater, who looked as though he'd cheerfully consume a whole lamb at a sitting, was incredulous. "What *do* you eat?"

"Tonight I'm having a nut-and-soybean casserole," the little lawyer said. He blew on the check to dry the ink, folded it, and put it away. "Nuits-St.-Georges should do nicely with it," he said. "Or perhaps a good bottle of Chambertin."

≡

The Chambertin and the nut-and-soybean casserole that it had so superbly complemented were but a memory four days later when a uniformed guard ushered the little lawyer into the cell where Evans Wheeler awaited him. The lawyer, neatly turned out in a charcoal-gray-flannel suit with a nipped-in waist, a blue shirt, and a navy tie with a below-the-knot design, contrasted sharply in appearance with his prospective client. Wheeler, as awkwardly tall and thin as a young Lincoln, wore striped overalls and a denim shirt. His footwear consisted of a pair of chain-store running shoes. The lawyer wore highly polished cordovan loafers.

And yet, Ehrengraf noted, the young man was poised enough in his casual costume. It suited him, even to the stains and chemical burns on the overalls and the ragged patch on one elbow of the workshirt.

"Mr. Ehrengraf," said Wheeler, extending a bony hand. "Pardon the uncomfortable surroundings. They don't go out of their way to make suspected mass murderers comfortable." He smiled ruefully. "The newspapers are calling it the crime of the century."

"That's nonsense," said Ehrengraf. "The century's not over yet. But the crime's unarguably a monumental one, sir, and the evidence against you would seem to be particularly damning."

"That's why I want you on my side, Mr. Ehrengraf."

"Well," said Ehrengraf.

"I know your reputation, sir. You're a miracle worker, and it looks as though that's what I need."

"What you very likely need," Ehrengraf said, "is a master of delaying tactics. Someone who can stall your case for as long as possible to let some of the heat of the moment be discharged. Then, when public opinion has lost some of its fury, he can arrange for you to plead guilty to homicide while of unsound mind. Some sort of insanity defense might work, or might at least reduce the severity of your sentence."

"But I'm innocent, Mr. Ehrengraf."

"I wouldn't presume to say otherwise, Mr. Wheeler, but I don't know that I'd be the right person to undertake your defense. I charge high fees, you see, which I collect only in the event that my clients are entirely exonerated. This tends to limit the nature of my clients."

"To those who can afford you."

"I've defended paupers. I've defended the poor as a court-appointed attorney and I volunteered my services on behalf of a poet. But in the ordinary course of things, my clients seem to have two things in common. They can afford my high fees. And, of course, they're innocent."

"I'm innocent."

"Indeed."

"And I'm a long way from being a pauper, Mr. Ehrengraf. You know that I used to work for Triage Corporation, the manufacturer of Darnitol."

"So I understand."

"You know that I resigned six months ago."

"After a dispute with your employer."

"Not a dispute," Wheeler said. "I told him where he could resituate a couple of test tubes. You see, I was in a position to make the suggestion, although I don't know that he was in a position to follow it. On my own time I'd developed a process for extenuating polymers so as to produce a variable-stress polymer capable of withstanding—"

Wheeler went on to explain just what the oxypolymer was capable of withstanding, and Ehrengraf wondered what the young man was talking about. He tuned in again to hear him say, "And so my royalty on the process in the first year will be in excess of six hundred thousand dollars, and I'm told that's only the beginning."

"Only the beginning," said Ehrengraf.

"I haven't sought other employment because there doesn't seem to be much point in it, and I haven't changed my lifestyle because I'm happy as I am. But I don't want to spend the rest of my life in prison, Mr. Ehrengraf, nor do I want to escape on some technicality and be loathed by my neighbors for the remainder of my days. I want to be exonerated and I don't care what it costs me."

"Of course you do," said Ehrengraf, drawing himself stiffly erect. "Of course you do. After all, son, you're innocent."

"Exactly."

"Although," Ehrengraf said with a sigh, "your innocence may be rather tricky to prove. The evidence—"

"Is overpowering."

"Like Nuits-St.-Georges with veal. A search of your workroom revealed a full container of Cydonex. You denied ever having seen it before."

"Absolutely."

Ehrengraf frowned. "I wonder if you mightn't have purchased it as an aid to pest control. Rats are troublesome. One is always being plagued by rats in one's cellar, mice in one's pantry, squirrels in one's attic—"

"And bats in one's belfry, I suppose, but my house has always been comfortingly free of vermin. I keep a cat. I suppose that helps."

"I'm sure it must, but I don't know that it helps your case. You seem to have purchased Cydonex from a chemical-supply house on North Division Street, where your signature appears in the poison-control ledger."

"A forgery."

"No doubt, but a convincing one. Bottles of Darnitol, some unopened, others with a single Cydonex-filled capsule added, were found on a closet shelf in your home. They seem to be from the same lot as those used to murder thirteen people."

"I was framed, Mr. Ehrengraf."

"And cleverly so, it would seem."

"I never bought Cydonex. I never so much as heard of Cydonex, not until people started dying of it."

"Oh? You worked for the plastics company that discovered the substance. That was before you took employment with the Darnitol people."

"It was also before Cydonex was invented. You know those dogs people mount on their dashboards and the head bobs up and down when you drive?"

"Not when I drive," Ehrengraf said.

"Nor I either, but you know what I mean. My job was finding a way to make the dogs' eyes more realistic. If you had a dog bobbing on your dashboard, would you even want the eyes to be more realistic?"

"Well," said Ehrengraf.

"Exactly. I quit that job and went to work for the Darnitol folks, and then my previous employer found a better way to kill rats, and so it looks as though I'm tied into the murders in two different ways. But actually I've never had anything to do with Cydonex and I've never so much as swallowed a Darnitol, let alone paid good money for that worthless snake oil."

"Someone bought those pills."

"Yes, but it wasn't—"

"And someone purchased that Cydonex. And forged your name to the ledger."

"Yes."

"And planted the bottles of Darnitol on drugstore and supermarket shelves after fatally tampering with their contents."

"Yes."

"And waited for the random victims to buy the pills, to work their way through the bottle until they ingested the deadly capsule, and to die in agony. And planted evidence to incriminate you."

"Yes."

"And made an anonymous call to the police to put them on your trail." Ehrengraf permitted himself a slight smile, one that did not quite reach his eyes. "And there he made his mistake," he said. "He could have waited for nature to take its course, just as he had already waited for the Darnitol to do its deadly work. They were checking on ex-employees of Triage Corporation. They'd have gotten to you sooner or later. But he wanted to hurry matters along, and that proves you were framed, sir, because who but the man who framed you would ever think to have called the police?"

"So the very phone call that got me on the hook serves to get me off the hook?"

"Ah," said Ehrengraf, "would that it were that easy."

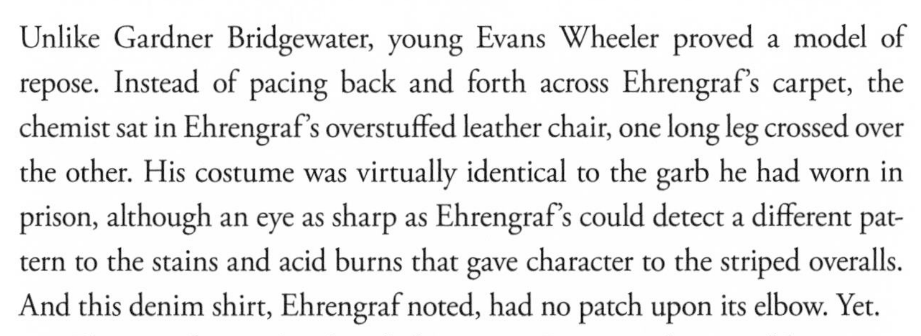

Unlike Gardner Bridgewater, young Evans Wheeler proved a model of repose. Instead of pacing back and forth across Ehrengraf's carpet, the chemist sat in Ehrengraf's overstuffed leather chair, one long leg crossed over the other. His costume was virtually identical to the garb he had worn in prison, although an eye as sharp as Ehrengraf's could detect a different pattern to the stains and acid burns that gave character to the striped overalls. And this denim shirt, Ehrengraf noted, had no patch upon its elbow. Yet.

Ehrengraf, seated at his desk, wore a Dartmouth-green blazer over tan flannel slacks. As was his custom on such occasions, his tie was once again the distinctive Caedmon Society cravat.

"Ms. Joanna Pellatrice," said Ehrengraf. "A teacher of seventh- and eighth-grade social studies at Kenmore Junior High School.

Unmarried, twenty-eight years of age, and living alone in three rooms on Deerhurst Avenue."

"One of the killer's first victims."

"That she was. The very first victim, in point of fact, although Ms. Pellatrice was not the first to die. Her murderer took one of the capsules from her bottle of Darnitol, pried it open, disposed of the innocent if ineffectual powder within, and replaced it with the lethal Cydonex. Then he put it back in her bottle, returned the bottle to her medicine cabinet or purse, and waited for the unfortunate woman to get a headache or cramps or whatever impelled her to swallow the capsules."

"Whatever it was," Wheeler said, "they wouldn't work."

"This one did, when she finally got to it. In the meantime, her intended murderer had already commenced spreading little bottles of joy all over the metropolitan area, one capsule to each bottle. There was danger in doing so, in that the toxic nature of Darnitol might come to light before Ms. Pellatrice took her pill and went to that big classroom in the sky. But he reasoned, correctly it would seem, that a great many persons would die before Darnitol was seen to be the cause of death. And indeed this proved to be the case. Ms. Pellatrice was the fourth victim, and there were to be many more."

"And the killer—"

"Refused to leave well enough alone. His name is George Grodek, and he'd had an affair with Ms. Pellatrice, although married to another teacher all the while. The affair evidently meant rather more to Mr. Grodek than it did to Ms. Pellatrice. He had made scenes, once at her apartment, once at her school during a midterm examination. The newspapers describe him as a disappointed suitor, and I suppose the term's as apt as any."

"You say he refused to leave well enough alone."

"Indeed," said Ehrengraf. "If he'd been content with depopulating the area and sinking Triage Corporation, I'm sure he'd have gotten away with it. The police would have had their hands full checking people with a grudge against Triage, known malcontents and mental cases, and the sort of chaps who get themselves into messes of that variety. But he has a neat sort of mind, has Mr. Grodek, and so he managed to learn of your existence and decided to frame you for the chain of murders."

Ehrengraf brushed a piece of lint from his lapel. "He did a workmanlike job," he said, "but it broke down on close examination. That signature in the control book did turn out to be a forgery, and matching forgeries of your name—trials, if you will—turned up in a notebook hidden away in a dresser drawer in his house."

"That must been hard for him to explain."

"So were the bottles of Darnitol in another drawer of the dresser. So was the Cydonex, and so was the little machine for filling and closing the capsules, and a whole batch of broken capsules which evidently represented unsuccessful attempts at pill-making."

"Funny he didn't flush it all down the toilet."

"Successful criminals become arrogant," Ehrengraf explained. "They believe themselves to be untouchable. Grodek's arrogance did him in. It led him to frame you, and to tip the police to you."

"And your investigation did what no police investigation could do."

"It did," said Ehrengraf, "because mine started from the premise of innocence. If you were innocent, someone else was guilty. If someone else was guilty and had framed you, that someone must have had a motive for the crime. If the crime had a motive, the murderer must have had a reason to kill one of the specific victims. And if that was the case, one had only to look to the victims to find the killer."

"You make it sound so simple," said Wheeler. "And yet if I hadn't had the good fortune to engage your services, I'd be spending the rest of my life in prison."

"I'm glad you see it that way," Ehrengraf said, "because the size of my fee might otherwise seem excessive." He named a figure, whereupon the chemist promptly uncapped a pen and wrote out a check.

"I've never written a check for so large a sum," he said reflectively.

"Few people have."

"Nor have I ever gotten greater value for my money. How fortunate I am that you believed in me, in my innocence."

"I never doubted it for a moment."

"You know who else claims to be innocent? Poor Grodek. I understand the madman's screaming in his cell, shouting to the world that he never killed anyone." Wheeler flashed a mischievous smile. "Perhaps he should hire you, Mr. Ehrengraf."

"Oh, dear," said Ehrengraf. "No, I think not. I can sometimes work miracles, Mr. Wheeler, or what have the appearance of miracles, but I can work them only on behalf of the innocent. And I don't think the power exists to persuade me of poor Mr. Grodek's innocence. No, I fear the man is guilty, and I'm afraid he'll be forced to pay for what he's done." The little lawyer shook his head. "Do you know Longfellow, Mr. Wheeler?"

"Old Henry Wadsworth, you mean? 'By the shores of Gitche Gumee, by the something Big-Sea-Water'? That Longfellow?"

"The shining Big-Sea-Water," said Ehrengraf. "Another client reminded me of 'The Village Blacksmith,' and I've been looking into Longfellow lately. Do you care for poetry, Mr. Wheeler?"

"Not too much."

"'In the world's broad field of battle, In the bivouac of Life, Be not like dumb, driven cattle! Be a hero in the strife!'"

"Well," said Evans Wheeler, "I suppose that's good advice, isn't it?"

"None better, sir. 'Let us then be up and doing, with a heart for any fate; still achieving, still pursuing, learn to labor and to wait.'"

"Ah, yes," said Wheeler.

"'Learn to labor and to wait,'" said Ehrengraf. "That's the ticket, eh? 'To labor and to wait.' Longfellow, Mr. Wheeler. Listen to the poets, Mr. Wheeler. The poets have the answers, haven't they?" And Ehrengraf smiled, with his lips and with his eyes.

The EHRENGRAF Affirmation

"The red rose whispers of passion,
And the white rose breathes of love;
O, the red rose is a falcon,
And the white rose is a dove."

—John Boyle O'Reilly

I've been giving this a lot of thought," Dale McCandless said. "Actually, there's not much you can do around here but think."

Ehrengraf glanced around the cell, wondering to what extent it was conducive to thought. There were, it seemed to him, no end of other activities to which the little room would lend itself. There was a bed on which you could sleep, a chair in which you could read, a desk at which you might write the Great American Jailhouse Novel. There was enough floor space to permit pushups or sit-ups or running in place, and, high overhead, there was the pipe that supported the light fixture, and that would as easily support you, should you contrive to braid strips of bedsheet into a rope and hang yourself.

Ehrengraf rather hoped the young man wouldn't attempt the last-named pursuit. He was, after all, innocent of the crimes of which he stood accused. All you had to do was look at him to know as much, and the little lawyer had not even needed to do that. He'd been convinced of his client's innocence the instant the young man had become a client. No client of Martin H. Ehrengraf could ever be other than innocent. This was more than a presumption for Ehrengraf. It was an article of faith.

"What I think would work for me," young McCandless continued, "is the good old Abuse Excuse."

"The Abuse Excuse?"

"Like those rich kids in California," McCandless said. "My father was all the time beating up on me and making me do stuff, and I was in fear for my life, blah blah blah, so what else could I do?"

"Your only recourse was to whip out a semiautomatic assault rifle," Ehrengraf said, "and empty a clip into the man."

"Those clips empty out in no time at all. You touch the trigger and the next thing you know the gun's empty and there's fifteen bullets in the target."

"Fortunately, however, you had another clip."

"For Mom," McCandless agreed. "Hey, she was as abusive as he was."

"And you were afraid of her."

"Sure."

"Your mother was in a wheelchair," Ehrengraf said gently. "She suffered from multiple sclerosis. Your father walked with a cane as the result of a series of small strokes. You're a big, strapping lad. Hulking, one might even say. It might be difficult to convince a jury that you were in fear for your life."

"That's a point."

"If you'd been living with your parents," Ehrengraf added, "people might wonder why you didn't just move out. But you had in fact moved out some time ago, hadn't you? You have your own home on the other side of town."

Dale McCandless nodded thoughtfully. "I guess the only thing to do," he said, "is play the Race Card."

"The Race Card?"

"Racist cops framed me," he said. "They planted the evidence."

"The evidence?"

"The assault rifle with my prints on it. The blood spatters on my clothes. The gloves."

"The gloves?"

"They found a pair of gloves on the scene," McCandless said. "But I'll tell you something nobody else knows. If I were to try on those gloves, you'd see that they're actually a size too small for me. I couldn't get my hands into them."

"And racist cops planted them."

"You bet."

Ehrengraf put the tips of his fingers together. "It's a little difficult for me to see the racial angle here," he said gently. "You're white, Mr. McCandless."

"Yeah, right."

"And both your parents were white. And all of the police officers involved in the investigation are white. All of your parents' known associates are white, and everyone living in that neighborhood is white. If there were a woodpile at the scene, I've no doubt we'd find a Caucasian in it. This is an all-white case, Mr. McCandless, and I just don't see a race card for us to play."

"Rats," Dale McCandless said. "If the Abuse Excuse is out and there's no way to play the Race Card, I don't know how I'm going to get out of this. The only thing left is the Rough Sex defense, and I suppose you've got some objection to that, too."

"I think it would be a hard sell," Ehrengraf said.

"I was afraid you'd say that."

"It seems to me you're trying to draw inspiration from some high-profile cases that don't fit the present circumstances. But there is one case that does."

"What's that?"

"Miss Elizabeth Borden," Ehrengraf said.

McCandless frowned in thought. "Elizabeth Borden," he said. "I know Elsie Borden, she's married to Elmer and she gives condensed milk. Even if Elsie's short for Elizabeth, I don't see how—"

"Lizzie," Ehrengraf pointed out, "is also short for Elizabeth."

"Lizzie Borden," McCandless said, and his eyes lit up. "Oh, yeah. A long time ago, right? Took an axe and gave her mother forty whacks?"

"So they say."

"'And when she saw what she had done, she gave her father forty-one.' I remember the poem."

"Everybody remembers the poem," Ehrengraf said. "What everyone forgets is that Miss Borden was innocent."

"You're kidding. She got off?"

"Of course she did," Ehrengraf said. "The jury returned a verdict of Not Guilty. And how could they do otherwise, Mr. McCandless? The woman was innocent." He allowed himself a small smile. "Even as you and I," he said.

═══

"Innocent," Dale McCandless said. "What a concept."

"All my clients are innocent," Ehrengraf told him. "That's what makes my work so gratifying. That and the fees, of course."

"Speaking of which," McCandless said, "you can set your mind to rest on that score. Even if they wind up finding me guilty and that keeps me from inheriting from my parents, I've still got more than enough to cover whatever you charge me. See, I came into a nice piece of change when my grandmother passed away."

"Is that what enabled you to buy a house of your own?"

"It set me up pretty good. I've got the house and I've got money in the bank. See, I was her sole heir, so when she took a tumble on the back staircase, everything she had came to me."

"She fell down the stairs?"

McCandless nodded. "They ought to do something about that staircase," he said. "Three months earlier, my grandfather fell down those same stairs and broke his neck."

"And left all his money to your grandmother," Ehrengraf said.

"Right."

"Who in turn left it to you."

"Yeah. Handy, huh?"

"Indeed," said Ehrengraf. "It must have been a frightening thing for an old woman, tumbling down a flight of stairs."

"Maybe not," McCandless said. "According to the autopsy, she was already dead when she fell. So what probably happened is she had a heart attack while she was standing at the top of the stairs and never felt a thing."

"A heart attack."

"Or a stroke or something," McCandless said carefully. "Or maybe she was sleeping and a pillow got stuck over her face and suffocated her."

"The pillow just got stuck on top of her face?"

"Well, she was old," McCandless said. "Who knows what could happen?"

"And then, after the pillow smothered her, how do you suppose she got from her bed to the staircase?"

"Sleepwalking," McCandless said.

"Of course," said Ehrengraf. "I should have thought of that."

"My parents lived in this ranch house," McCandless said. "Big sprawling thing, lots of square footage but all of it on one level. No basement and no attic." He sighed. "In other words, no stairs." He shook his head ruefully. "Point is, there was never any problem about my grandparents' death, so I've got some money of my own. So you don't have to worry about your fee."

Ehrengraf drew himself up straight. He was a small man, but his perfect posture and impeccably-tailored raw silk suit lent him stature beyond his height. "There will be no fee," he said, "unless you are found innocent."

"Huh?"

"My longstanding policy, Mr. McCandless. My fees are quite considerable, but they are payable only in the event that my client is exonerated. As it happens, I rarely see the inside of a courtroom. My clients are innocent, and their innocence always wins out in the long run. I do what I can toward that end, often working behind the scenes. And, when charges are dropped, when the real killer confesses, when my client's innocence has been demonstrated to the satisfaction of the legal system, then and only then do I profit from my efforts on his behalf."

McCandless was silent for a long moment. At length he fixed his eyes on the little lawyer. "We got ourselves a problem," he said. "See, just between you and me, I did it."

"With stairs," young McCandless was saying, "it might have been entirely different. Especially with Mom in the wheelchair. Good steep flight of stairs and it's a piece of cake. Instead I went out and got the gun, and then I bought the gloves."

"Gloves?"

"A size too small," McCandless said. "To leave at the crime scene. I thought—well, never mind what I thought. I guess I wasn't thinking too clearly. Hey, that reminds me. You think maybe a Dim Cap defense would turn the trick?"

"Innocent by reason of diminished capacity?"

"Yeah. See, I did a couple of lines of DTT before I went out and bought the gloves."

"Do you mean DDT? The insecticide?"

"Naw, DTT. It's short for di-tetra thiazole, it's a tranquilizer for circus animals, but if you snort it it sort of mellows you out. What I could do, though, is I could forget about the DTT and tell people I ate a Twinkie."

Court TV, Ehrengraf thought, had a lot to answer for. "You got the gun," he prompted his client, "and you bought the gloves..."

"And I went over there and did what I had to do. But of course I don't remember that part."

"You don't?"

McCandless shook his head. "Not a thing, from the time I parked the car in their driveway until I woke up hours later in my own bed. See, I never remember. I don't remember doing my grandparents, either. It's all because of the EKG."

"I'm not sure I follow you," said Ehrengraf, rather understating the matter. "You had an electrocardiogram?"

"That's for your heart, isn't it? My heart's fine. No, EKG's this powder, you roll it up and smoke it. I couldn't tell you what the initials stand for, but it was originally developed as a fertilizer for African violets. They had to take it off the market when they found out what it did to people."

"What does it do?"

"I guess it gets you high," McCandless said, "but I don't know for sure. See, what happens is you take it and you black out. It's the same story every time I smoke it. I light up, I take the first puff, and the next thing I remember I'm waking up in my own bed hours later. So I couldn't tell you what it feels like. All I know is what it lets me do while I'm operating behind it. And so far it's let me do my grandparents and my mother and father."

"I knew it," Ehrengraf said.

"How's that?"

"I knew you were innocent," he said. "I knew it. Mr. McCandless, you have no memory whatsoever of any of those killings, is that what you're telling me?"

"Yeah, but—"

"You may have intended to do those persons harm. But it was so much against your nature that you had to ingest a dangerous controlled substance in order to gird yourself for the task. Is that correct?"

"Well, more or less, but—"

"And you have no recollection of committing any crimes whatsoever. You believe yourself to be guilty, and as a result you are in a jail cell charged with a hideous crime. Do you see the problem, sir? The problem is not what you have done, because in fact you have done nothing. The problem is what you believe."

McCandless looked at him.

"If you don't believe in your own innocence," Ehrengraf demanded, "how can the rest of the world believe in it? Your thoughts are powerful, Mr. McCandless. And right now your own negative thoughts are damning you as a murderer."

"But—"

"You must affirm your innocence, sir."

"Okay," McCandless agreed. "'I'm innocent.' How's that?"

"It's a start," Ehrengraf said. He opened his briefcase, drew out a yellow legal pad, produced a pen. "But it takes more than a simple declaration to change your own thoughts on the matter. What I want you to do is affirm your innocence in writing."

"Just write 'I'm innocent' over and over?"

"It's a little more complicated than that." Ehrengraf uncapped the pen and drew a vertical line down the center of the page. "Here's what you do," he said. "Over here on the left you write 'I am completely innocent.' Then on the right you immediately write down the first negative response to that sentence that pops into your mind."

"Fair enough." McCandless took the pad and pen. *I am completely innocent*, he wrote in the left-hand column. *What a load of crap*, he wrote at once on the right.

"Excellent," Ehrengraf assured him. "Now keep going, but with a different response each time."

"Just keep going?"

"Until you get to the bottom of the page," Ehrengraf said.

The pen raced over the paper, as McCandless no sooner proclaimed his complete innocence than he dashed off a repudiation of it. When he'd reached the bottom of the page, Ehrengraf took the pad from him.

I am completely innocent/I murdered both my parents

I am completely innocent/Killed Grandma and Grampa

I am completely innocent/I deserve the gas chamber

I am completely innocent/I'm guilty as sin

I am completely innocent/They ought to hang me

I am completely innocent/I'm a murderer

I am completely innocent/I killed a girl last year and there wasn't even any money in it for me

I am completely innocent/I'm a born killer

I am completely innocent/I am bad, bad, bad!

"Excellent," Ehrengraf said.

"You think so? If the District Attorney got a hold of that…"

"Ah, but he won't, will he?" Ehrengraf crumpled the paper, stuffed it into a pocket, handed the legal pad back to his client. "All of those negative thoughts," he explained, "have been festering in your mind and soul, preventing you from believing in your own untarnished innocence. By letting them surface this way, we can stamp them out and affirm your own true nature."

"My own true nature's nothing to brag about," McCandless said.

"That's your negativity talking," Ehrengraf told him. "At heart you're an innocent child of God." He pointed to the legal pad, made scribbling motions in the air. "You've got work to do," he said.

"I hope you got another of those yellow pads there," Dale McCandless said. "It's a funny thing. I was never much of a writer, and in school it was torture for me to write a two-page composition for English class. You know, '*How I Spent My Summer Vacation*?'"

Ehrengraf, who could well imagine how a young McCandless might have spent his summer vacation, was diplomatically silent.

"But this time around," McCandless said, "I've been writing up a storm. What's it been, five days since you got me started? Well, I ran through that pad you gave me, and I got one of the guards to bring me this little notebook, but I like the pads better. Here, look at what I wrote this morning."

Ehrengraf unfolded a sheet of unlined white paper. McCandless had drawn a line down its center, writing his affirmation over and over again in the left-hand column, jotting down his responses to the right.

I am completely innocent/I've been in trouble all my life
I am completely innocent/Maybe it wasn't always my fault
I am completely innocent/I don't remember doing anything bad
I am completely innocent/In my heart I am
I am completely innocent/How great it would be if it was true!

"You've come a long way," Ehrengraf told his client. "You see how the nature of your responses is changing."

"It seems like magic," McCandless said.

"The magic of affirmation."

"All along, I would just write down the first thing that popped into my head. But the old bad stuff just stopped popping in."

"You cleared it away."

"I don't know what I did," McCandless said. "Maybe I just wore it out. But it got to the point where it didn't seem natural to write that I was a born killer."

"Because you're not."

"I guess."

"And how do you feel now, Mr. McCandless? Without a pen in your hand, just talking face to face? Are you innocent of the crimes of which you stand accused?"

"Maybe."

"Maybe?"

"It's almost too much to hope for," the young man said, "but maybe I am. I could be, couldn't I? I really could be."

Ehrengraf beamed. "Indeed you are," he said, "and it's my job to prove it. And yours—" he opened his briefcase, provided his client with a fresh legal pad "—yours to further affirm that innocence until there is no room in your consciousness for doubt and negativity. You've got work to do, Mr. McCandless. Are you up for it?"

Eagerly, McCandless reached for the pad.

"Little Bobby Bickerstaff," McCandless said, shaking his head in wonder.

Ehrengraf's hand went to the knot of his necktie, adjusting it imperceptibly. The tie was that of the Caedmon Society, and Ehrengraf was not entitled to wear it, never having been a member of that organization. It was, however, his invariable choice for occasions of triumph, and this was just such an occasion.

"I never would have dreamed it," McCandless said. "Not in a million years."

"You knew him, then?"

"We went to grade school together. In fact we were in the same class until I got held back. You know something? *That's* hard to believe, too."

"That you'd be held back? I must say I find it hard to believe myself. You're an intelligent young man."

"Oh, it wasn't for that. It was for deportment. You know, talking in class, throwing chalk."

"High spirits," Ehrengraf said.

"Setting fires," McCandless went on. "Breaking windows. Doing cars."

"Doing cars?"

"Teachers' cars," the young man explained. "Icepicking the tires, or sugaring the gas tank, or keying the paint job. Or doing the windows."

"Bricking them," Ehrengraf suggested.

"I suppose you could call it that. That's what's hard to believe, Mr. Ehrengraf. That I did those things."

"I see."

"I used to be like that," he said, and frowned in thought. "Or maybe I just used to *think* I was that way, and that's why I did bad things."

"Ah," Ehrengraf said.

"All along I was innocent," McCandless said, groping for the truth. "But I didn't know it, I had this belief I was bad, and when I was a little kid it made me do bad things."

"Precisely."

"And I got in trouble, and they blamed me even when I didn't do anything bad, and that convinced me I was really bad, bad clear to the bone. And...and..."

The youth put his head in his hands and sobbed.

"There, there," Ehrengraf said softly, and clapped him on the shoulder.

After a moment McCandless got hold of himself and said, "But little Bobby Bickerstaff. I can't get over it."

"He killed your parents," Ehrengraf said.

"It's so hard to believe. I always thought of him as a little goody-goody."

"A nice quiet boy," Ehrengraf said.

"Yeah, well, those are the ones who lose it, aren't they? They pop off one day and the neighbors can't believe it, same as I can't believe it myself about Bobby. What was the name of the couple he killed?"

"Roger and Sheila Capstone."

"I didn't know them," McCandless said, "but they lived in the same neighborhood as my folks, in the same kind of house. And was she in a wheelchair the same as my mom?"

"It was Mr. Capstone who was wheelchair-bound," Ehrengraf said. "He'd been crippled in an automobile accident."

"Poor guy. And little Bobby Bickerstaff emptied a clip into him, and another into his wife."

"So it seems."

"Meek little Bobby. Whacked them both, then went into the bathroom and wrote something on the mirror."

"It was Mrs. Capstone's dressing table mirror," Ehrengraf said. "And he used her lipstick to write his last message."

"'This is the last time. God forgive me.'"

"His very words."

"And then he put on the woman's underwear," McCandless said, "or maybe he put it on before, who knows, and then he popped a fresh clip in his gun and stuck the business end in his mouth and got off a burst. Must have made some mess."

"I imagine it did."

McCandless shook his head in amazement. "Little Bobby," he said. "Mr. Straight Arrow. Cops searched his place afterward, house he grew up in, what did they find? All these guns and knives and dirty magazines and stuff."

"It happens all the time," Ehrengraf said.

"Other stuff, too. Some things that must have been stolen from my parents' house, not that anybody had even noticed they were missing. Some jewelry of my mom's and a sterling silver flask with my dad's initials engraved on it. I don't think I ever even knew he had a flask, but how many are you going to find engraved W. R. McC.?"

"It could only have been his."

"Well, sure. But what really wrapped it up was the diary. From what I heard, most of it was sketchy, just weird stuff that was going through his mind. But the entry the day after my parents died, that was something else."

"It was a little vague as well," Ehrengraf said, "but quite conclusive all the same. He told how he'd gone to your parents' home and found you passed out in a chair."

"From the EKG, it must have been."

"He thought about killing all three of you. Instead he gunned down both your parents, making sure that you and your clothes were spattered with their blood, then wiped his prints off the empty gun and pressed it into your hands."

"Bobby's mom was crippled," McCandless remembered. "I remember kids used to say we ought to be friends because of it. Like him and me were in the same boat."

"But you weren't friends."

"Are you kidding? A hood like me team up with a goody-goody like Bobby Bickerstaff?" His expression turned thoughtful. "Except it turns out I was innocent all along, so I wasn't such a hood after all. And Bobby wasn't such a goody-goody."

"No."

"In fact," McCandless said, "he might have had something to do with his own parents' death. Bobby was still a kid at the time. They weren't too clear on what happened, whether it was a suicide pact or the old man committed a mercy killing and then killed himself afterward. I guess everybody figured it amounted to the same thing. But now..."

"Now there's suspicion that Bobby may have done it."

"I suppose he could have. There's a pattern, isn't there? His mom was crippled, my mom was in a wheelchair, and this Mr. Capstone was more of the same. Maybe the shock of what happened to his folks drove him around the bend, or maybe he was the one responsible for what happened to them to start with, and the other two murders were just a way of re-enacting the crime. I wonder which it was."

"I doubt we'll ever know," Ehrengraf said gently.

"I guess not," McCandless said. "What we do know is *I* didn't kill anybody, and I already knew that, thanks to you. Bobby killed my parents, and my grandparents both had simple accidents. That's what the police decided at the time, and it was only my own negative thoughts about myself that led me to believe I had anything to do with their deaths."

"That's it," Ehrengraf said, delighted. "You're absolutely right."

"I'll tell you, Mr. Ehrengraf, this business with affirmations is pretty amazing stuff. I mean, I did some bad things over the years. Let's face it, I pulled some mean stuff. But do you know why?"

"Tell me, Dale."

"I did it because I thought I was bad. I mean, if you're a bad person, what do you do? You do bad things. I thought I was bad, so I did some bad things."

"'Give a dog a bad name—'"

"And he'll bite you," McCandless said. "And I did, in a manner of speaking, but I never killed anybody. And now that I know I'm innocent, I'll be a changed human being entirely."

"A productive member of society."

"Well, I don't know about productive," McCandless said. "I mean, face it, I'm a rich man. Between what I had from my grandmother and what I stand to inherit from my parents, I can live a life of ease." He grinned. "Even after I pay your fee, I'm still set for life."

"An enviable position to be in."

"So I may not knock myself out being productive," McCandless went on. "I may just focus on having fun."

"Boys will be boys," said Ehrengraf.

"You said it. I'll work on my suntan, I'll see that the bar's well stocked, I'll round up a couple of totally choice babes. Get some good drugs, plenty of tasty food in case anybody gets the munchies, and next thing you know—"

"Drugs," Ehrengraf said.

"Hey, it's like you said, Mr. Ehrengraf. Boys will be boys."

"Suppose you got hold of some of that EKG."

"Suppose I did? I'm innocent, Mr. Ehrengraf. You're the one showed me how to see that. Anything I do, drunk or sober, straight or loaded, it's going to be innocent. So what have I got to worry about?"

He grinned disarmingly, but Ehrengraf was not disarmed. "I'm not sure EKG is a good idea for you," he said carefully.

"You could be right. But sooner or later it'll be around, and I won't be able to resist it. But so what? I can handle it."

Ehrengraf reached for the yellow legal pad, turned to a clean sheet, drew a line down the center of the page. "Here," he said, handing the pad to McCandless. "This time I'd like you to work with a different affirmation."

"How about 'I am a perfect child of God?' I sort of like the sound of that one."

"Let's try something a little more specific," Ehrengraf suggested. "Write, 'I am through with EKG, now and forever.'"

McCandless frowned, shrugged, took the pad and started writing. Ehrengraf, watching over his shoulder, read the responses as his client wrote them.

I am through with EKG, now and forever/You must be kidding

I am through with EKG, now and forever/I love the way it makes me crazy

I am through with EKG, now and forever/I'll never give it up

I am through with EKG, now and forever/What harm does it do?

I am through with EKG, now and forever/I couldn't resist it

"We have our work cut out for us," Ehrengraf said. "But that only shows how deep the thought goes. Look at the self-image you had earlier, and look how you managed to turn it around."

"I know I'm innocent."

"And the world has changed to reflect the change in your own mental landscape. Once you became clear on your innocence, proof of it began to manifest in the world around you."

"I think I see what you mean."

Ehrengraf handed the legal pad back to his client. The process would work, he assured himself. Soon the mere thought of ingesting EKG would be anathema to young Dale McCandless.

And that, Ehrengraf thought, would be all to the good. Because he had a feeling the world would be a kinder and gentler place for all if the innocent Mr. McCandless never ingested that particular chemical again.

The EHRENGRAF Reverse

"How does it happen, tell me,
That I lie here unmarked, forgotten,
While Chase Henry, the town drunkard,
Has a marble block, topped by an urn,
Wherein Nature, in a mood ironical,
Has sown a flowering weed?"

—Edgar Lee Masters

"I didn't do it," Blaine Starkey said.

"Of course you didn't."

"Everyone thinks I did it," Starkey went on, "and I guess I can understand why. But I'm innocent."

"Of course you are."

"I'm not a murderer."

"Of course you're not."

"Not this time," the man said. "Mr. Ehrengraf, it's not supposed to matter whether a lawyer thinks his client is guilty or innocent. But it matters to me. I really am innocent, and it's important that you believe me."

"I do."

"I don't know why it's so important," Starkey said, "but it just is, and—" He paused, and seemed to register for the first time what Ehrengraf had been saying all along. His big open face showed puzzlement.

"You do?"

"Yes."

"You believe I'm innocent."

"Absolutely."

"That's pretty amazing, Mr. Ehrengraf. Nobody else believes me."

Ehrengraf regarded his client. Indeed, if you looked at the man's record you could hardly avoid presuming him guilty. But once you turned your gaze into his cornflower blue eyes, how could you fail to recognize the innocence gleaming there?

Even if you didn't believe the man, how would you have the nerve to tell him so? Blaine Starkey was, to say the least, an imposing presence. When you saw him on the television screen, catching a pass and racing downfield, breaking tackles as effortlessly as a politician breaks his word, you didn't appreciate the sheer size of him. All the men on the field were huge, and your eye learned to see them as normal.

In a jail cell, across a little pine table, you began to realize just how massive a man Blaine Starkey was. He stood as many inches over six feet as Ehrengraf stood under it, and was big in the shoulders and narrow in the waist, with thighs like tree trunks and arms like—well, words failed Ehrengraf. The man was enormous.

"The whole world thinks I killed Claureen," Starkey said, "and it's not hard to see why. I mean, look at my stats."

His stats? Thousands of yards gained rushing. Hundreds of passes caught. No end of touchdowns scored. Ehrengraf, who was more interested in watching the action on the field than in crunching the numbers, knew nevertheless that the big man's statistics were impressive.

He also knew Starkey meant another set of stats.

"I mean," the man said, "it's not like this never happened before. Three women, three coffins. Hell, Mr. Ehrengraf, if I was a hockey player they'd call it the hat trick."

"But it's not hockey," Ehrengraf assured him, "and it's not football, either. You're an innocent man, and there's no reason you should have to pay for a crime you didn't commit."

"You really think I'm innocent," Starkey said.

"Absolutely."

"That's what everybody's supposed to presume, until it's proved otherwise. Is that what you mean? That I'm innocent for the time being, far as the law's concerned?"

Ehrengraf shook his head. "That's not what I mean."

"You mean innocent no matter what the jury says."

"I mean exactly what you meant earlier," the little lawyer said. "You didn't kill your wife. You're entirely innocent of her death, and the jury should never be in a position to say anything on the subject, because you should never be brought to trial. You're an innocent man, Mr. Starkey."

The football player took a deep breath, and Ehrengraf was surprised that there was any air left in the cell. "That's just so hard for me to believe."

"That you're innocent?"

"Hell, I *know* I'm innocent," Starkey said. "What's hard to believe is that *you* believe it."

But how could Ehrengraf believe otherwise? He fingered the knot in his deep blue necktie and reflected on the presumption of innocence—not the one which had long served as a cardinal precept of Anglo-American jurisprudence, but a higher, more personal principle. The Ehrengraf presumption. Any client of Martin H. Ehrengraf's was innocent. Not until proven guilty, but until the end of time.

But he didn't want to get into a philosophical discussion with Blaine Starkey. He kept it simple, explaining that he only represented the innocent.

The football player took this in. His face fell. "Then if you change your mind," he said, "you'll drop me like a hot rock. Is that about right?"

"I won't change my mind."

"If you get to thinking I'm guilty—"

"I'll never think that."

"But—"

"We're wasting time," Ehrengraf told him. "We both know you're innocent. Why dispute a point on which we're already in agreement?"

"I guess I really found the one man who believes me," Starkey said. "Now where are we gonna find twelve more?"

"It's my earnest hope we won't have to," Ehrengraf said. "I rarely see the inside of a courtroom, Mr. Starkey. My fees are very high, but I have to earn them in order to receive them."

Starkey scratched his head. "That's what I'm not too clear on."

"It's simple enough. I take cases on a contingency basis. I don't get paid unless and until you walk free."

"I've heard of that in civil cases," Starkey said, "but I didn't know there were any criminal lawyers who operated that way."

"As far as I know," Ehrengraf said, "I am the only one. And I don't depend on courtroom pyrotechnics. I represent the innocent, and through my efforts their innocence becomes undeniably clear to all concerned. Then and only then do I collect my fee."

And what would that be? Ehrengraf named a number.

"Whole lot of zeroes at the end of it," the football player said, "but it's nothing to the check I wrote out for the Proud Crowd. Five of them, and they spent close to a year on the case, hiring experts and doing studies and surveys and I don't know what else. A man can make a lot of money if he can run the ball and catch a pass now and then. I guess I can afford your fee, plus whatever the costs and expenses come to."

"The fee is all-inclusive," Ehrengraf said.

"If that's so," Starkey said, "I'd say it's a bargain. And I only pay if I get off?"

"And you will, sir."

"If I do, I don't guess I'll begrudge you your fee. And if I don't, do I get my retainer back? Not that I'd have a great use for it, but—"

"There'll be no retainer," Ehrengraf said smoothly. "I like to earn my money before I receive it."

"I never heard of anybody like you, Mr. Ehrengraf."

"There isn't anyone like me," Ehrengraf said. "I've been thrilled to watch you play, and I don't believe there's anyone like you, either. We're both unique."

"Well," Starkey said.

"And yet you're charged with killing your wife," Ehrengraf said smoothly. "Hard to believe, but there it is."

"Not so hard to believe. I've been tried twice for murder and got off both times. How many times can a man kill his wife and get away with it?"

It was a good question, but Ehrengraf chose not to address it. "The first woman wasn't your wife," he said.

"My girlfriend. Kate Waldecker. I was in my junior year at Texas State." He looked at his hands. "We were in bed together, and one way or another my hands got around her neck."

"You engaged Joel Daggett as your attorney, if I remember correctly."

"The Bulldog," Starkey said fondly. "He came up with this rough sex defense. Brought in witnesses to testify that Kate liked to be hurt while she was making love, liked to be choked half to death. Made her out to be real kinky, and a tramp in the bargain. I have to say I felt sorry for her folks. They were in tears through the trial." He sighed. "But what else could he do? I mean, I got out of bed and called the cops, told everybody I did it. Daggett got the confession suppressed, but there was still plenty of evidence that I did it. He had to find a way to keep it from being murder."

"And he was successful. You were found not guilty."

"Yeah, but that was bullshit. Kate didn't like it rough. Fact, she was always telling me to slow down, to be gentler with her." He frowned. "Hard to say what happened that night. We'd been arguing earlier, but I thought I was over being mad about that. Next thing I knew she was dead and I was unhooking my hands from around her throat. I always figured the steroids I was taking might have had something to do with it, but maybe not. Maybe I just got carried away and killed her. Anyway, Daggett saw to it that I got away with it."

"You didn't go back for your senior year."

"No, I turned pro right after the trial. I would have liked to get my degree, but I didn't figure they'd cheer as hard for me after I'd killed a fellow student. Besides, I had a big legal bill to pay, and that's where the signing bonus went."

"You went with the Wranglers."

"I was their first-round draft choice and I was with them for four seasons. Born in Texas, went to school in Texas, and I thought I'd play my whole career in Texas. Married a Texas girl, too. Jacey was beautiful, even if she was hell on wheels. High-strung, you know? Threw a glass ashtray at me once, hit me right here on the cheekbone. Another inch and I might have lost an eye." He shook his head. "I figured we'd get divorced sooner or later. I just wanted to stay married to her until I got tired of, you know, goin' to bed with her. But I never did get tired of her that way, or divorced from her, either, and then the next thing I knew she was dead."

"She killed herself."

"They found her in bed, with bruises on her neck. And they picked me up at the country club, where I was sitting by myself in the bar, hitting the bourbon pretty good. They hauled me downtown and charged me with murder."

"You didn't give a statement."

"Didn't say a word. I knew that much from my first trial. Of course I couldn't get the Bulldog this time, on account of he was dead. Lee Waldecker walked up to him in a restaurant in Austin about a year after my acquittal, shot him in front of a whole roomful of people. I guess he never got over the job Daggett did on his sister's reputation. He said he could almost forgive me, because all I did was kill Kate, but what Daggett did to her was worse than murder."

"He's still serving his sentence, isn't he?"

"Life without parole. A jury might have cut him loose, or slapped him on the wrist with a short sentence, but he went and pleaded guilty. Said he did it in front of witnesses on purpose, so he wouldn't have some lawyer twisting the truth."

"So you got a whole team of lawyers," Ehrengraf said. "The press made up a name for them."

"The Proud Crowd. Each one thought he was the hottest thing going, and they spent a lot of time just cutting each other apart. And they sure weren't shy about charging for their services. But I'd made a lot of money all those years, and I figured to make a lot more if I kept on playing, and the Wranglers wanted to make sure I had the best possible defense."

"Not rough sex this time."

"No, I don't guess you can get by with that more than once. What's funny is that Jacey *did* like it rough. Matter of fact, there weren't too many ways she didn't like it. If the Bulldog was around, and if I hadn't already used that defense once already, rough sex would have had me home free. Jacey was everything Daggett tried to make Kate look like, and there would have been dozens of people willing to swear to it."

"As it turned out," Ehrengraf said, "it was suicide, wasn't it? And the police tampered with the evidence?"

"That was the line the Proud Crowd took. There were impressions on her neck from a large pair of hands, but they dug up a forensics expert who testified that they'd been inflicted after death, like some-body'd strangled her after she'd already been dead for some time. And they had another expert testify that there were rope marks on her neck, underneath the hand prints, suggesting she'd hanged herself and been cut down. There were fibers found on and near the corpse, and another defense expert matched them to a rope that had been retrieved from a Dumpster. And they found residue of talcum powder on the rope, and another expert testified that it was the same kind of talcum powder Jacey used, and had used the day of her death."

"So many experts," Ehrengraf murmured.

"And every damn one of 'em sent in a bill," Starkey said, "but I can't complain, because they earned their money. According to the Proud Crowd, Jacey hanged herself. I came home, saw her like that, and just couldn't deal with it. I cut her down and tried to revive her, then lost it and went to the club to brace myself with a few drinks while I figured out what to do next. Meantime, a neighbor called the cops, and as far as they were concerned I was this old boy who made a couple million dollars a year playing a kid's game, and already put one wife in the ground and got away with it. So they made sure I wouldn't get away with it a second time by taking the rope and losing it in a Dumpster, and pressing their hands into her neck to make it look like manual strangulation."

"And is that how it happened?"

Starkey rolled his eyes. "How it happened," he said, "is we were having an argument, and I took this hunk of rope and put it around her neck and strangled the life out of her."

Ehrengraf winced.

"Don't worry," his client went on. "Nobody can hear us, and what I tell you's privileged anyway, and besides it'd be double jeopardy, because twelve people already decided they believed the Proud Crowd's version. But they must have been the only twelve people in the country who bought it, because the rest of the world figured out that I did it. And got away with it again."

"You were acquitted."

"I was and I wasn't," he said. "Legally I was off the hook, but that didn't mean I got my old life back. The Wranglers put out this press release about how glad they were that justice was served and an innocent man exonerated, but nobody would look me in the eye. First chance they got, they traded me."

"And you've been with the Mastodons ever since."

"And I love it here," he said. "I don't even mind the winters. Back when I played for the Wranglers I hated coming up here for late-season games, but I got so I liked the cold weather. You get used to it."

Ehrengraf, a native, had never had to get used to the climate. But he nodded anyway.

"At first," Starkey said, "I thought about quitting. But I owed all this money to the Proud Crowd, and how was I going to earn big money off a football field? I lost my endorsements, you know. I had this one commercial, I don't know if you remember it, where Minnie Mouse is sitting on my lap and sort of flirting with me."

"You were selling a toilet-bowl cleaner," Ehrengraf recalled.

"Yeah, and when they dropped me I figured that meant I wasn't good enough to clean toilets. But what choice did they have? People were saying things like you could just about see the marks on Minnie's neck. Long story short, no more commercials. So what was I gonna do but play?"

"Of course."

"Besides, I was in my mid-twenties and I loved the game. Now it's ten years later and I still love it. I got Cletis Braden breathing down my neck, trying to take my job away, but I figure it's gonna be a few more years before he can do it. Love the city, live here year round, wouldn't want to live anywhere else. Love the house I bought. Love the people, even love the winters. Snow? What's so bad about snow?"

"It's pretty," Ehrengraf said.

"Damn pretty. It's around for a while and then it melts. And then it's gone." He made a fist, opened it, looked at his palm. "Gone, like everything else. Like my career. Like my damn life."

For a moment Ehrengraf thought the big man might burst into tears, and rather hoped he would not. The moment passed, and the little lawyer suggested they talk about the late Mrs. Starkey.

"Which one? No, I know you mean Claureen. Local girl, born and bred here. Went away to college and got on the cheerleading squad. I guess she got to know the players pretty good." He rolled his eyes. "Came back home, went to work teaching school, but she found a way to hang around football players. I'd been here a couple of years by then, and the Mastodons don't lack for feminine companionship, so I was doing okay in that department. But it was time to get married, and I figured she was the one."

Romeo and Juliet, Ehrengraf thought. Tristan and Isolde. Blaine and Claureen.

"And it was okay," Starkey said. "No kids, and that was disappointing, but we had a good life and we got along okay. I never ran around on her here in town, and what you do on the road don't count. Everybody knows that."

"And the day she died?"

"We had a home game coming up with the Leopards. I went out for a couple of beers after practice, but I left early because Clete Braden showed up and joined us and I can tire of his company pretty quick. I drove around for an hour or two. Went over to Boulevard Mall to see what was playing at the multiplex. They had twelve movies, but nothing I wanted to see. I thought I'd walk around the mall, maybe buy something, but I can't go anywhere without people recognizing me, and sometimes I just don't want to deal with that. I drove around some more and went home."

"And discovered her body."

"In the living room, crumpled up on the rug next to the fireplace, bareass naked and stone cold dead. First thing I thought was she had a fainting spell. She'd get lightheaded if she went too long between meals, and she'd been trying to drop a few pounds. Don't ask me why, she looked fine to me, but you know women."

"Nobody does," Ehrengraf said.

"Well, that's the damn truth, but you know what I mean. Anyway, I knelt down and touched her, and right away I knew she was dead. And then I saw her head was all bloody, and I thought, well, here we go again."

"You called the police."

"Last thing I wanted to do. Wanted to get in the car and just drive, but I knew not to do that. And I wanted to pour a stiff drink and I didn't let myself do that, either. I called 911 and I sat in a chair, and when the cops came I let 'em in. I didn't answer any of their questions. I barely heard them. I just kept my mouth shut, and they brought me here, and I wound up calling you."

"And it's good you did," Ehrengraf told him. "You're innocent, and soon the whole world will know it."

Three days later the two men faced one another in the same cell across the same little table. Blaine Starkey looked weary. Part of it was the listless sallowness one saw in imprisoned men, but Ehrengraf noted as well the sag of the shoulders, the lines around the mouth. He was wearing the same clothes he'd worn at their previous meeting. Ehrengraf, in a three-piece suit with a banker's stripe and a tie striped like a coral snake, wondered not for the first time if he ought to dress down on such occasions, to put his client at ease. As always, he decided that dressing down was not his sort of thing.

"I've done some investigation," he reported. "Your wife's blood sugar was low."

"Well, she wasn't eating. I told you that."

"The Medical Examiner estimated the time of death at two to four hours before you reported discovering her body."

"I said she felt cold to the touch."

"She died," Ehrengraf said, "sometime after football practice was over for the day. The prosecution is going to contend that you had time before you met your teammates for drinks—"

"To race home, hit Claureen upside the head, and then rush out to grab a beer?"

"—or afterward, during the time you were driving around and trying to decide on a movie."

"I had the time then," Starkey allowed, "but that's not how I spent it."

"I know that. When you got home, was the door locked?"

"Sure. We keep it so it locks when you pull it shut."

"Did you use your key?"

"Easier than ringing the bell and waiting. Her car was there, so I knew she was home. I let myself in and keyed in the code so the burglar alarm wouldn't go off, and then I walked into the living room, and you know the rest."

"She died," Ehrengraf said, "as a result of massive trauma to the skull. There were two blows, one to the temple, the other to the back of the head. The first may have resulted from her fall, when she struck herself upon the sharp corner of the fireplace surround. The second blow was almost certainly inflicted by a massive bronze statue of a horse."

"She picked it out," Starkey said. "It was French, about a hundred and fifty years old. I didn't think it looked like any horse a reasonable man would want to place a bet on, but she fell in love with it and said it'd be perfect on the mantle."

Ehrengraf fingered the knot of his tie. "Your wife was nude," he said.

"Maybe she just got out of the shower," the big man said. "Or you know what I bet it was? She was on her way *to* the shower."

"By way of the living room?"

"If she was on the stair machine, which was what she would do when she decided she was getting fat. An apple for breakfast and an enema for lunch, and hopping on and off the stair machine all day long. She'd exercise naked if she was warm, or if she wore a sweat suit she'd leave it there in the exercise room and parade through the house naked."

"Then it all falls into place," Ehrengraf said. "She wasn't eating enough and was exercising excessively. She completed an ill-advised session on the stair climber, shed her exercise clothes if in fact she'd been wearing any in the first place, and walked through the living room on her way to the shower."

"She'd do that, all right."

"Her blood sugar was dangerously low. She got dizzy, and felt faint. She started to fall, and reached out to steady herself, grabbing the bronze horse. Then she lost consciousness and fell, dragging the horse from its perch on the mantelpiece as she did so. She went down hard, hitting her forehead on the bricks, and the horse came down hard as well, striking her on the head. And, alone in the house, the unfortunate woman died an accidental death."

"That's got to be it," Starkey said. "I couldn't put it together. All I knew was I didn't kill her. You can push that argument, right? You can get me off?"

But Ehrengraf was shaking his head. "If you had spent the twelve hours preceding her death in the company of an archbishop and a Supreme Court justice," he said, "and if both of those worthies were at your side when you discovered your wife's body, then it might be possible to advance that theory successfully in court."

"But—"

"The whole world thinks of you as a man who got away with murder twice already. Do you think a jury is going to let you get away with it a third time?"

"The prosecution can't introduce either of those earlier cases as evidence, can they?"

"They can't even mention them," Ehrengraf said, "or it's immediate grounds for a mistrial. But why mention them when everyone already knows all about them? If they didn't know to begin with, they're reading the full story every day in the newspaper and watching clips of your two trials on television."

"Then it's hopeless."

"Only if you go to trial."

"What else can I do? I could try fleeing the country, but where would I hide? What would I do, play professional football in Iraq or North Korea? And I can't even try, because they won't let me out on bail."

Ehrengraf put the tips of his fingers together. "I've no intention of letting this case go to trial," he said. "I don't much care for the whole idea of leaving a man's fate in the hands of twelve people, not one of them clever enough to get out of jury duty."

Puzzlement showed in Starkey's face.

"I remember a run you made against the Jackals," Ehrengraf said. "The quarterback gave the ball to that other fellow—"

"Clete Braden," Starkey said heavily.

"—and he began running to his right, and you were running toward him, and he handed the ball to you, and you swept around to the left, after all the Jackals had shifted over to stop Braden's run to the right."

Starkey brightened. "I remember the play," he said. "The reverse. When it works, it's one of the prettiest plays in football."

"It worked against the Jackals."

"I ran it in. Better than sixty yards from scrimmage, and once I was past midfield no one had a shot at me."

Ehrengraf beamed. "Ah, yes. The reverse. It is something to see, the reverse."

It was a new Blaine Starkey that walked into Martin Ehrengraf's office. He was dressed differently, for one thing, his double-breasted tan suit clearly the work of an accomplished tailor, his maroon silk shirt open at its flowing collar, his cordovan wing tips buffed to a high sheen. His skin had thrown off the jailhouse pallor and glowed with the ruddy health of a life lived outdoors. There was a sparkle in his eyes, a spring in his step, a set to his shoulders. It did the little lawyer's heart good to see him.

He was holding a football, passing it from hand to hand as he approached Ehrengraf's desk. How small it looked, Ehrengraf thought, in those big hands. And with what ease could those hands encircle a throat...

Ehrengraf pushed the thought aside, and his hand went to his necktie. It was his Caedmon Society tie, his inevitable choice on triumphant occasions, and a nice complement to his cocoa brown blazer and fawn slacks.

"The game ball," Starkey announced, reaching to place it on the one clear spot on the little lawyer's cluttered desk. "They gave it to me after Sunday's game with the Ocelots. See, all the players signed it. All but Cletis Braden, but I don't guess he'll be signing too many game balls from here on."

"I shouldn't think so."

"And here's where I wrote something myself," he said, pointing.

Ehrengraf read: "*To Marty Ehrengraf, who made it all possible. From your buddy, Blaine Starkey.*"

"Marty," Ehrengraf said.

Starkey lowered his eyes. "I didn't know about that," he admitted. "If people called you Marty or Martin or what. I mean, all I ever called you was 'Mr. Ehrengraf.' But with sports memorabilia, people generally like it to look like, you know, like them and the athlete are good buddies. Do they call you Marty?"

They never had, but Ehrengraf merely smiled at the question and took the ball in his hands. "I shall treasure this," he said simply.

"Here's something else to treasure," Starkey said. "It's autographed, too."

"Ah," Ehrengraf said, and took the check, and raised his eyebrows at the amount. It was not the sum he had mentioned at their initial meeting. This had happened before, when a client's gratitude gave way to innate penuriousness, and Ehrengraf routinely made short work of such attempts to reduce his fee. But this check was for more than he had demanded, and that had *not* happened before.

"It's a bonus," Starkey said, anticipating the question. "I don't know if there's such a thing in your profession. We get them all the time in the NFL. It's not insulting, is it? Like tipping the owner of the restaurant? Because I surely didn't intend it that way."

Ehrengraf, nonplussed, shook his head. "Money is only insulting," he managed, "when there's too little of it." He beamed, and stowed the check in his wallet.

"I'll tell you," Starkey said, "writing checks isn't generally my favorite thing in the whole world, but I couldn't have been happier when I was writing out that one. Couple of weeks ago I was the worst thing since Jack the Ripper, and now I'm everybody's hero. Who was it said there's no second half in the game of life?"

"Scott Fitzgerald wrote something along those lines," Ehrengraf said, "but I believe he phrased it a little differently."

"Well, he was wrong," Starkey said, "and you proved it. And who would have dreamed it would turn out this way?"

Ehrengraf smiled.

"Clete Braden," Starkey said. "I knew the sonofabitch was after my job, but who'd have guessed he was after my wife, too? I swear I never had a clue those two were slipping around behind my back. It's still hard to believe Claureen was cheating on me when I wasn't even on a road trip."

"They must have been very clever in their deceit."

"But stupid at the same time," Starkey said. "Taking her to a motel and signing in as Mr. and Mrs. Cleveland Brassman. Same initials, plus he used his own handwriting on the registration card. Made up a fake address but used his real license plate number, just switching two digits around." He rolled his eyes. "And then leaving a pair of her panties in the room. Where was it they found them? Wedged under the chair cushion or some such?"

"I believe so."

"All that time and the maids never found them. I guess they don't knock themselves out cleaning the rooms in a place like that, but I'd still have to call it a piece of luck the panties were still there."

"Luck," Ehrengraf agreed.

"And no question they were hers, either. Matched the ones in her dresser drawer, and had her DNA all over 'em. It's a wonderful thing, DNA."

"A miracle of modern forensic science."

"Why'd they even go to a motel in the first place? Why not take her to his place? He wasn't married, he had women in and out of his apartment all the time."

"Perhaps he didn't want to be seen with her."

"Long as I wasn't the one doing the seeing, what difference could it make?"

"None," Ehrengraf said, "unless he was afraid of what people might remember afterward."

Starkey thought about that. Then his eyes widened. "He planned it all along," he said.

"It certainly seems that way."

"Wanted to make damn sure he got my job, by seeing to it that I wasn't around to compete for it. He didn't just lose his temper when he smashed her head with that horse. It was all part of the plan—kill her and frame me for it."

"Diabolical," Ehrengraf said.

"That explains what he wrote on that note," Starkey said. "The one they found at the very back of her underwear drawer, arranging to meet that last day after practice. 'Make sure you burn this,' he wrote. And he didn't even sign it. But it was in his handwriting."

"So the experts say."

"And on a piece of his stationery. The top part was torn off, with his name and address on it, but it was the same brand of bond paper. It would have been nice if they could have found the piece he tore off and matched them up, but I guess you can't have everything."

"Perhaps they haven't looked hard enough," Ehrengraf murmured. "There was another note as well, as I recall. One that she wrote."

"On one of the printed memo slips with her name on it. A little love note from her to him, and he didn't have the sense to throw it out. Carried it around in his wallet."

"It was probably from early in their relationship," Ehrengraf said, "and very likely he'd forgotten it was there."

"He must have. It surprised the hell out of him when the cops went through his wallet and there it was."

"I imagine it did."

"He must have gone to my house straight from practice. Wouldn't have been a trick to get her out of her clothes, seeing as he'd been managing that all along. 'My, Claureen, isn't that a cute little horse.' 'Yes, it's French, it's over a hundred years old.' 'Is that right? Let me just get the feel of it.' And that's the end of Claureen. A shame he didn't leave a fingerprint or two on the horse just for good measure."

"You can't have everything," Ehrengraf said. "Wiping his prints off the horse would seem to be one of the few intelligent things Mr. Braden managed. But they can make a good case against him without it. Of course much depends on his choice of an attorney."

"Maybe he'll call you," Starkey said with a wink. "But I guess that wouldn't do him any good, seeing as you only represent the innocent. What I hear, he's fixing to put together a Proud Crowd of his own. Figure they'll get him off?"

"It may be difficult to convict him," Ehrengraf allowed, "but he's already been tried and found guilty in the court of public opinion."

"The league suspended him, and of course he's off the Mastodons' roster. But what's really amazing is the way everybody's turned around as far as I'm concerned. Before, I was a man who got away with killing two women, but they could live with that as long as I could put it all together on the field. Then I killed a third woman, and they flat out hated me, and then it turns out I *didn't* kill Claureen, I was an innocent man framed for it, and they did a full-scale turnaround, and the talk is maybe I really *was* innocent those other two times, just the way the two juries decided I was. All of a sudden there's a whole lot of people telling each other the system works and feeling real good about it."

"As well they might," said Ehrengraf.

"They cheer you when you catch a pass," Starkey said philosophically, "and they boo you when you drop one. Except for you, Mr.

Ehrengraf, there wasn't a person around who believed I didn't do it. But you did, and you figured out how the evidence showed Claureen's death was accidental. Low blood sugar, too much exercise, and she got dizzy and fell and pulled the horse down on top of her."

"Yes."

"And then you figured out they'd never buy that, true or false. So you dug deeper."

"It was the only chance," Ehrengraf said modestly.

"And they might not buy that Claureen killed herself by accident, but they loved the idea that she was cheating on me and Clete killed her so I'd be nailed for it."

"The Ehrengraf reverse."

"How's that?"

"The Ehrengraf reverse. When the evidence is all running one way, you hand off the ball and sweep around the other end." He spread his hands. "And streak down the sideline and into the end zone."

"Touchdown," Starkey said. "We win, and Braden's the goat and I'm the hero."

"As you clearly were on Sunday."

"I guess I had a pretty decent game."

"Eight pass receptions, almost two hundred yards rushing—yes, I'd say you had a good game."

"Say, were those seats okay?"

"Row M on the fifty-yard line? They were the best seats in the stadium."

"It was a beautiful day for it, too, wasn't it? And I couldn't do a thing wrong. Oh, next week I'll probably fumble three times and run into my own blockers a lot, but I'll have this one to remember."

Ehrengraf took the game ball in his hands. "And so will I," he said.

"Well, I wanted you to have a souvenir. And the bonus, well, I got more money coming in these days than I ever figured to see. Every time the phone rings it's another product endorsement coming my way, and I don't have to wait too long between rings, either. Hey, speaking of the reverse, how'd you like the one we ran Sunday?"

"Beautiful," Ehrengraf said fervently. "A work of art."

"You know, I was thinking of you when they called it in the huddle. Fact, when the defense was on the field I asked the coach if we couldn't run that play. Would have served me right if I'd been dumped for a loss, but that's not what happened."

"You gained forty yards," Ehrengraf said, "and if that one man hadn't missed a downfield block, you'd have had another touchdown."

"Well, it's a pretty play," Blaine Starkey said. "There's really nothing like the reverse."

The EHRENGRAF Settlement

"Let me have men about me that are fat,
Sleek-headed men, and such as sleep a-nights.
Yond Cassius has a lean and hungry look.
He thinks too much. Such men are dangerous."

—William Shakespeare

Ehrengraf, his mind abuzz with uplifting thoughts, left his car at the curb and walked the length of the flagstone path to Millard Ravenstock's imposing front door. There was a large bronze door-knocker in the shape of an elephant's head, and one could lift and lower the animal's hinged proboscis to summon the occupants.

Or, as an alternative, one could ring the doorbell by pressing the recessed mother-of-pearl button. Ehrengraf fingered the knot in his tie, with its alternating half-inch stripes of scarlet and Prussian blue, and brushed a speck of lint from the lapel of his gray flannel suit. Only then, having given both choices due consideration, did he touch the elephant's trunk, before opting instead for the bell-push.

Moments later he was in a paneled library, seated in a leather club chair, with a cup of coffee at hand. He hadn't managed more than two sips of the coffee before Millard Ravenstock joined him.

"Mr. Ehrengraf," the man said, giving the honorific just enough emphasis to suggest how rarely he employed it. Ehrengraf could believe it; this was a man who would call most people by their surnames, as if all the world's inhabitants were members of his household staff.

"Mr. Ravenstock," said Ehrengraf, with an inflection that was similar but not identical.

"It was good of you to come to see me. In ordinary circumstances I'd have called at your offices, but—"

A shrug and a smile served to complete the sentence.

In ordinary circumstances, Ehrengraf thought, the man would not have come to Ehrengraf's office, because there'd have been no need for their paths to cross. Had Millard Ravenstock not found himself a person of interest in a murder investigation, he'd have had no reason to summon Ehrengraf, or Ehrengraf any reason to come to the imposing Nottingham Terrace residence.

Ehrengraf simply observed that the circumstances were not ordinary.

"Indeed they are not," said Ravenstock. His chalk-striped navy suit was clearly the work of a custom tailor, who'd shown skill in flattering his client's physique. Ravenstock was an imposing figure of a man, stout enough to draw a physician's perfunctory warnings about cholesterol and type-two diabetes, but still well on the right side of the current national standard for obesity. Ehrengraf, who maintained an ideal weight with no discernible effort, rather agreed with Shakespeare's Caesar, liking to have men about him who were fat.

"'Sleek-headed men, and such as sleep a-nights.'"

"I beg your pardon?"

Had he spoken aloud? Ehrengraf smiled, and waved a dismissive hand. "Perhaps," he said, "we should consider the matter that concerns us."

"Tegrum Bogue," Ravenstock said, pronouncing the name with distaste. "What kind of a name is Tegrum Bogue?"

"A distinctive one," Ehrengraf suggested.

"Distinctive if not distinguished. I've no quarrel with the surname. One assumes it came down to him from the man who provided half his DNA. But why would anyone name a child Tegrum? With all the combinations of letters available, why pick those six and arrange them in that order?" He frowned. "Never mind, I'm wandering off-topic. What does his name matter? What's relevant is that I'm about to be charged with his murder."

"They allege that you shot him."

"And the allegation is entirely true," Ravenstock said. "I don't suppose you like to hear me admit as much, Mr. Ehrengraf. But it's pointless for me to deny it, because it's the plain and simple truth."

Ehrengraf, whose free time was largely devoted to the reading of poetry, moved from Shakespeare to Oscar Wilde, who had pointed out that the truth was rarely plain, and never simple. But he kept himself from quoting aloud.

"It was self-defense," Ravenstock said. "The man was hanging around my property and behaving suspiciously. I confronted him. He responded in a menacing fashion. I urged him to depart. He attacked me. Then and only then did I draw my pistol and shoot him dead."

"Ah," said Ehrengraf.

"It was quite clear that I was blameless," Ravenstock said. His high forehead was dry, but he drew a handkerchief and mopped it just the same. "The police questioned me, as they were unquestionably right to do, and released me, and one detective said offhand that I'd done the right thing. I consulted with my attorney, and he said he doubted charges would be brought, but that if they were he was confident of a verdict of justifiable homicide."

"And then things began to go wrong."

"Horribly wrong, Mr. Ehrengraf. But you probably know the circumstances as well as I do."

"I try to keep up," Ehrengraf allowed. "But let me confirm a few facts. You're a member of the Nottingham Vigilance Committee."

"The name's unfortunate," Ravenstock said. "It simply identifies the group as what it is, designed to keep a watchful eye over our neighborhood. This is an affluent area, and right across the street is Delaware Park. That's one of the best things about living here, but it's not an unmixed blessing."

"Few blessings are," said Ehrengraf.

"I'll have to think about that. But the park—it's beautiful, it's convenient, and at the same time people lurk there, some of them criminous, some of them emotionally disturbed, and all of them just a stone's throw from our houses."

There was a remark that was trying to occur to Ehrengraf, something about glass houses, but he left it unsaid.

"Police protection is good here," Ravenstock continued, "but there's a definite need for a neighborhood watch group. Vigilance—well, you hear that and you think *vigilante*, don't you?"

"One does. This Mr. Bogue—"

"Tegrum Bogue."

"Tegrum Bogue. You'd had confrontations with him before."

"I'd seen him on my property once or twice," Ravenstock said, "and warned him off."

"You'd called in reports of his suspicious behavior to the police."

"A couple of times, yes."

"And on the night in question," Ehrengraf said, "he was not actually on your property. He was, as I understand it, two doors away."

"In front of the Gissling home. Heading north toward Meadow Road, there's this house, and then the Robert Townsend house, and then Madge and Bernard Gissling's. So that would be two doors away."

"And when you shot him, he fell dead on the Gisslings' lawn."

"They'd just resodded."

"That very day?"

"No, a month ago. Why?"

Ehrengraf smiled, a maneuver that had served him well over the years. "Mr. Bogue—that would be Tegrum Bogue—was unarmed."

"He had a knife in his pocket."

"An inch-long penknife, wasn't it? Attached to his key ring?"

"I couldn't say, sir. I never saw the knife. The police report mentioned it. It was only an inch long?"

"Apparently."

"It doesn't sound terribly formidable, does it? But Bogue's was a menacing presence without a weapon in evidence. He was young and tall and vigorous and muscular and wild-eyed, and he uttered threats and put his hands on me and pushed me and struck me."

"You were armed."

"An automatic pistol, made by Gunnar & Swick. Their Kestrel model. It's registered, and I'm licensed to carry it."

"You drew your weapon."

"I did. I thought the sight of it might stop Bogue in his tracks."

"But it didn't."

"He laughed," Ravenstock recalled, "and said he'd take it away from me, and would stick it—well, you can imagine where he threatened to stick it."

Ehrengraf, who could actually imagine several possible destinations for the Kestrel, simply nodded.

"And he rushed at me, and I might have been holding a water pistol for all the respect he showed it."

"You fired it."

"I was taught never to show a gun unless I was prepared to use it."

"Five times."

"I was taught to keep on firing until one's gun was empty. Actually the Kestrel's clip holds nine cartridges, but five seemed sufficient."

"'To make assurance doubly sure,'" Ehrengraf said. "Stopping at five does show restraint."

"Well."

"And yet," Ehrengraf said, "the traditional argument that the gun simply went off of its own accord comes a cropper, doesn't it? It's a rare weapon that fires itself five times in rapid succession. As a member of the Nottingham Vigilantes—"

"The Vigilance Committee."

"Yes, of course. In that capacity, weren't you supposed to report Bogue's presence to the police rather than confront him?"

Ravenstock came as close to hanging his head as his character would allow. "I never thought to make the call."

"The heat of the moment," Ehrengraf suggested.

"Just that. I acted precipitously."

"A Mrs. Kling was across the street, walking her Gordon setter. She told police the two of you were arguing, and it seemed to be about someone's wife."

"He made remarks about my wife," Ravenstock said. "Brutish remarks, designed to provoke me. About what he intended to do to and with her, after he'd taken the gun away from me and put it, well—"

"Indeed."

"What's worse, Mr. Ehrengraf, is the campaign of late to canonize Tegrum Bogue. Have you seen the picture his family released to the press? He doesn't look very menacing, does he?"

"Only if one finds choirboys threatening."

"It was taken nine years ago," Ravenstock said, "when young Bogue was a first-form student at the Nichols School. Since then he shot up eight inches and put on forty or fifty pounds. I assure you, the cherub in the photo bears no resemblance to the hulking savage who attacked me steps from my own home."

"Unconscionable," Ehrengraf said.

"And now I'm certain to be questioned further, and very likely to be placed under arrest. My lawyer was nattering on about how unlikely it was that I'd ever have to spend a night in jail, and hinting at my pleading guilty to some reduced charge. That's not good enough."

"No."

"I don't want to skate on a technicality, my reputation in ruins. I don't want to devote a few hundred hours to community service. How do you suppose they'd have me serve my community, Mr. Ehrengraf? Would they send me across the street to pick up litter in the park? Or would they regard a stick with a sharp bit of metal at its end as far too formidable a weapon to be placed in my irresponsible hands?"

"These are things you don't want," Ehrengraf said soothingly. "And whyever should you want them? But perhaps you could tell me what it is that you *do* want."

"What I want," said Ravenstock, speaking as a man who generally got whatever it was that he wanted. "What I want, sir, is for all of this to go away. And my understanding is that you are a gentleman who is very good at making things go away."

Ehrengraf smiled.

THE EHRENGRAF Settlement

Ehrengraf gazed past the mound of clutter on his desk at his office door, with its window of frosted glass. What struck him about the door was that his client had not yet come through it. It was getting on for half past eleven, which made Millard Ravenstock almost thirty minutes late.

Ehrengraf fingered the knot in his tie. It was a perfectly symmetrical knot, neither too large nor too small, which was as it should be. Whenever he wore this particular tie, with its navy field upon which a half-inch diagonal stripe of royal blue was flanked by two narrower stripes, one of gold, the other vividly green—whenever he put it on, he took considerable pains to get the knot exactly right.

It was, of course, the tie of the Caedmon Society; Ehrengraf, not a member of that institution, had purchased the tie from a shop in Oxford's Cranham Close. He'd owned it for some years now, and had been careful to avoid soiling it, extending its useful life by reserving it for special occasions.

This morning had promised to be such an occasion. Now, as the minutes ticked away without producing Millard Ravenstock, he found himself less certain.

The antique Regulator clock on the wall, which lost a minute a day, showed the time as 11:42 when Millard Ravenstock opened the door and stepped into Ehrengraf's office. The little lawyer glanced first at the clock and then at his wristwatch, which read 11:48. Then he looked at his client, who looked not the least bit apologetic for his late arrival.

"Ah, Ehrengraf," the man said. "A fine day, wouldn't you say?"

You could see Niagara Square from Ehrengraf's office window, and a quick look showed that the day was as it had been earlier—overcast and gloomy, with every likelihood of rain.

"Glorious," Ehrengraf agreed.

Without waiting to be asked, Ravenstock pulled up a chair and settled his bulk into it. "Before I left my house," he said, "I went into my den, got out my checkbook, and wrote two checks. One, you'll be pleased to know, was for your fee." He patted his breast pocket. "I've brought it with me."

Ehrengraf was pleased. But, he noted, cautiously so. He sensed there was another shoe just waiting to be dropped.

"The other check is already in the mail. I made it payable to the Policemen's Benevolent Association, and I assure you the sum is a generous one. I have always been a staunch proponent of the police, Ehrengraf, if only because the role they play is such a vital one. Without them we'd have the rabble at our throats, eh?"

Ehrengraf, thought Ehrengraf. The *Mister*, present throughout their initial meeting, had evidently been left behind on Nottingham Terrace. Increasingly, Ehrengraf felt it had been an error to wear that particular tie on this particular morning.

"Yet I'd given the police insufficient credit for their insight and their resolve. Walter Bainbridge, a thorough and diligent policeman and, I might add, a good friend, pressed an investigation along lines others might have left unexplored. I've been completely exonerated, and it's largely his doing."

"Indeed," said Ehrengraf.

"The police dug up evidence, unearthed facts. That housewife who was raped and murdered three weeks ago in Orchard Park. I'm sure you're familiar with the case. The press called it the Milf Murder."

Ehrengraf nodded.

"It took place outside city limits," Ravenstock went on, "so it wasn't their case at all, but they went through the house and found an unwashed sweatshirt stuffed into a trashcan in the garage. Nichols School Lacrosse, it said, big as life. That's a curious expression isn't it? Big as life?"

"Curious," Ehrengraf said.

"Lacrosse seems to be the natural refuge of the preppy thug," Ravenstock said. "Can you guess whose DNA soiled that sweatshirt?"

Ehrengraf could guess, but saw no reason to do so. Nor did Ravenstock wait for a response.

"Tegrum Bogue's. He'd been on the team, and it was beyond question his shirt. He'd raped that young housewife and snapped her neck when he was through with her. And he had similar plans for Alicia."

"Your wife."

"Yes. I don't believe you've met her."

"I haven't had the pleasure."

The expression that passed over Ravenstock's face suggested that it was a pleasure Ehrengraf would have to live without. "She is a beautiful woman," he said. "And quite a few years younger than I. I suppose there are those who would refer to her as my trophy wife."

The man paused, waiting for Ehrengraf to comment, then frowned at the lawyer's continuing silence. "There are two ways to celebrate a trophy," he went on. "One may carry it around, showing it off at every opportunity. Or one may place it on a shelf in one's personal quarters, to be admired and savored in private."

"Indeed."

"Some men require that their taste have the approbation of others. They lack confidence, Ehrengraf."

Another pause. Some expression of assent seemed to be required of him, and Ehrengraf considered several, ranging from *Right on, dude* to *Most def.*

"Indeed," he said at length.

"But somehow Alicia caught his interest. He was one of the mob given to loitering in the park, and sometimes she'd walk Kossuth there."

"Kossuth," Ehrengraf said. "The Gordon setter?"

"No, of course not. I wouldn't own a Gordon. And why would anyone name a Gordon for Louis Kossuth? Our dog is a Viszla, and a fine and noble animal he is. He must have seen her walking Kossuth. Or—"

"Or?"

"I had my run-ins with him. In my patrol duty with the Vigilance Committee, I'd recommended that he and his fellows stay on their side of the street."

"In the park, and away from the houses."

"His response was not at all acquiescent," Ravenstock recalled. "After that I made a point of monitoring his activities, and phoned in the occasional police report. I'd have to say I made an enemy, Ehrengraf."

"I doubt you were ever destined to be friends."

"No, but I erred in making myself the object of his hostility. I think that's what may have put Alicia in his sights. I think he stalked me, and I think his reconnaissance got him a good look at Alicia, and of course to see her is to want her."

Ehrengraf, struck by the matter-of-fact tone of that last clause, touched the tips of two fingers to the Caedmon Society cravat.

"And the police found evidence of his obsession," Ravenstock said. "A roll of undeveloped film in his sock drawer, with photos for which my wife had served as an unwitting model. Crude fictional sketches, written in Bogue's schoolboy hand, some written in the third person, some in the first. Clumsy mini-stories relating in pornographic detail the abduction, sexual savaging, and murder of my wife. Pencil drawings to illustrate them, as ill-fashioned as his prose. The scenarios varied as his fantasies evolved. Sometimes there was torture, mutilation, dismemberment. Sometimes I was present, bound and helpless, forced to witness what was being done to her. And I had to watch because I couldn't close my eyes. I didn't read his filth, so I can't recall whether he'd glued my eyelids open or removed them surgically—"

"Either would be effective."

"Well," Ravenstock said, and went on, explaining that of course the several discoveries the police had made put paid to any notion that he, Millard Ravenstock, had done anything untoward, let alone criminal. He had not been charged, so there were no charges to dismiss, and what was at least as important was that he had been entirely exonerated in the court of public opinion.

"So you can see why I felt moved to make a generous donation to the Policemen's Benevolent Association," he continued. "I feel they earned it. And I'll find a way to express my private appreciation to Walter Bainbridge."

Ehrengraf waited, and refrained from touching his necktie.

"As for yourself, Ehrengraf, I greatly appreciate your efforts on my behalf, and have no doubt that they'd have proved successful had not Fate and the police intervened and done your job for you. And I'm sure you'll find this more than adequate compensation for your good work."

The check was in an envelope, which Ravenstock plucked from his inside breast pocket and extended with a flourish. The envelope was unsealed, and Ehrengraf drew the check from it and noted its amount, which was about what he'd come to expect.

"The fee I quoted you—"

"Was lofty," Ravenstock said, "but would have been acceptable had the case not resolved itself independent of any action on your part."

"I was very specific," Ehrengraf pointed out. "I said my work would cost you nothing unless your innocence was established and all charges dropped. But if that were to come about, my fee was due and payable in full. You do remember my saying that, don't you?"

"But you didn't *do* anything, Ehrengraf."

"You agreed to the arrangement I spelled out, sir, and—"

"I repeat, you did nothing, or if you did do anything it had no bearing on the outcome of the matter. The payment I just gave you is a settlement, and I pay it gladly in order to put the matter to rest."

"A settlement," Ehrengraf said, testing the word on his tongue.

"And no mere token settlement, either. It's hardly an insignificant amount, and my personal attorney hastened to tell me I'm being overly generous. He says all you're entitled to, legally and morally, is a reasonable return on whatever billable hours you've put in, and—"

"Your attorney."

"One of the region's top men, I assure you."

"I don't doubt it. Would this be the same attorney who'd have had you armed with a sharp stick to pick up litter in Delaware Park? After pleading you guilty to a murder for which you bore no guilt?"

Even as he marshaled his arguments, Ehrengraf sensed that they would prove fruitless. The man's mind, such as it was, was made up. Nothing would sway him.

≡

There was a time, Ehrengraf recalled, when he had longed for a house like Millard Ravenstock's—on Nottingham Terrace, or Meadow Road, or Middlesex. Something at once tasteful and baronial, something with pillars and a center hall, something that would proclaim to one and all that its owner had unquestionably come to amount to something.

True success, he had learned, meant one no longer required its accoutrements. His penthouse apartment at the Park Lane provided all the space and luxury he could want, and a better view than any house could offer. The building, immaculately maintained and impeccably staffed, even had a name that suited him; it managed to be as resolutely British as Nottingham or Middlesex without sounding pretentious.

And it was closer to downtown. When time and good weather permitted, Ehrengraf could walk to and from his office.

But not today. There was a cold wind blowing off the lake, and the handicappers in the weather bureau had pegged rain at even money. The little lawyer had arrived at his office a few minutes after ten. He made one phone call, and as he rang off he realized he could have saved himself the trip.

He went downstairs, retrieved his car, and returned to the Park Lane to await his guest.

≡

Ehrengraf, opening the door, was careful not to stare. The woman whom the concierge had announced as a Ms. Philips was stunning, and Ehrengraf worked to conceal the extent to which he was stunned. She was taller than Ehrengraf by several inches, with dark hair that someone very skilled had cut to look as though she took no trouble with it. She had great big Bambi eyes, the facial planes of a supermodel, and a full-lipped mouth that stopped just short of obscenity.

"Ms. Philips," Ehrengraf said, and motioned her inside.

"I didn't want to leave my name at the desk."

"I assumed as much. Come in, come in. A drink? A cup of coffee?"

"Coffee, if it's no trouble."

It was no trouble at all; Ehrengraf had made a fresh pot upon his return, and he filled two cups and brought them to the living room, where Alicia Ravenstock had chosen the Sheraton wing chair. Ehrengraf sat opposite her, and they sipped their coffee and discussed the beans and brewing method before giving a few minutes' attention to the weather.

Then she said, "You're very good to see me here. I was afraid to come to your office. There are enough people who know me by sight, and if word got back to him that I went to a lawyer's office, or even into a building where lawyers had offices—"

"I can imagine."

"I'm his alone, you see. I can have anything I want, except the least bit of freedom."

"Peter, Peter, pumpkin eater," Ehrengraf said, and when she looked puzzled he quoted the rhyme in full:

> "Peter, Peter, pumpkin eater,
> Had a wife and couldn't keep her.
> He put her in a pumpkin shell
> And there he kept her very well."

"Yes, of course. It's a nursery rhyme, isn't it?"

Ehrengraf nodded. "I believe it began life centuries ago as satirical political doggerel, but it's lived on as a rhyme for children."

"Millard keeps me very well," she said. "You've been to the pumpkin shell, haven't you? It's a very elegant one."

"It is."

"A sumptuous and comfortable prison. I suppose I shouldn't complain. It's what I wanted. Or what I thought I wanted, which may amount to the same thing. I'd resigned myself to it—or *thought* I'd resigned myself to it."

"Which may amount to the same thing."

"Yes," she said, and took a sip of coffee. "And then I met Bo."

"And that would be Tegrum Bogue."

"I thought we were careful," she said. "I never had any intimation that Millard knew, or even suspected." Her face clouded. "He was a lovely boy, you know. It's still hard for me to believe he's gone."

"And that your husband killed him."

"That part's not difficult to believe," she said. "Millard's cold as ice and harder than stone. The part I can't understand is how someone like him could care enough to want me."

"You're a possession," Ehrengraf suggested.

"Yes, of course. There's no other explanation." Another sip of coffee; Ehrengraf, watching her mouth, found himself envying the bone china cup. "It wouldn't have lasted," she said. "I was too old for Bo, even as Millard is too old for me. Mr. Ehrengraf, I had resigned myself to living the life Millard wanted me to live. Then Bo came along, and a sunbeam brightened up my prison cell, so to speak, and the life to which I'd resigned myself was now transformed into one I could enjoy."

"Made so by trysts with your young lover."

"Trysts," she said. "I like the word, it sounds permissibly naughty. But, you know, it also sounds like *tristesse*, which is sadness in French."

A woman who cared about words was very likely a woman on whom the charms of poetry would not be lost. Ehrengraf found himself wishing he'd quoted something rather more distinguished than *Peter, Peter, Pumpkin Eater.*

"I don't know how Millard found out about Bo," she said. "Or how he contrived to face him mere steps from our house and shoot him down like a dog. But there seemed to be no question of his guilt, and I assumed he'd have to answer in some small way for what he'd done. He wouldn't go to prison, rich men never do, but look at him now, Mr. Ehrengraf, proclaimed a defender of home and hearth who slew a rapist and murderer. To think that a sweet and gentle boy like Bo could have his reputation so blackened. It's heartbreaking."

"There, there," Ehrengraf said, and patted the back of her hand. The skin was remarkably soft, and it felt at once both warm and cool, which struck him as an insoluble paradox but one worth investigating. "There, there," he said again, but omitted the pat this time.

"I blame the police," she said. "Millard donates to their fund-raising efforts and wields influence on their behalf, and I'd say it paid off for him."

Ehrengraf listened while Alicia Ravenstock speculated on just how the police, led by a man named Bainbridge, might have constructed a post-mortem frame for Tegrum Bogue. She had, he was pleased to note, an incisive imagination. When she'd finished he suggested more coffee, and she shook her head.

"I have to end my marriage," she said abruptly. "There's nothing for it. I made a bad bargain, and for a time I thought I could live with it, and now I see the impossibility of so doing."

"A divorce, Mrs. Ravenstock—"

She recoiled at the name, then forced a smile. "Please don't call me that," she said. "I don't like being reminded that it's my name. Call me Alicia, Mr. Ehrengraf."

"Then you must call me Martin, Alicia."

"Martin," she said, testing the name on her pink tongue.

"It's not terribly difficult to obtain a divorce, Alicia. But of course you would know that. And you would know, too, that a specialist in matrimonial law would best serve your interests, and you wouldn't come to me seeking a recommendation in that regard."

She smiled, letting him find his way.

"A pre-nuptial agreement," he said. "He insisted you sign one and you did."

"Yes."

"And you've shown it to an attorney, who pronounced it iron-clad."

"Yes."

"You don't want more coffee. But would you have a cordial? Bénédictine? Chartreuse? Perhaps a Drambuie?"

"It's a Scotch-based liqueur," Ehrengraf said, after his guest had sampled her drink and signified her approval.

"I've never had it before, Martin. It's very nice."

"More appropriate as an after-dinner drink, some might say. But it brightens an afternoon, especially one with weather that might have swept in from the Scottish Highlands."

He might have quoted Robert Burns, but nothing came to mind. "Alicia," he said, "I made a great mistake when I agreed to act as your husband's attorney. I violated one of my own cardinal principles. I have made a career of representing the innocent, the blameless, the unjustly accused. When I am able to believe in a client's innocence, no matter how damning the apparent evidence of his guilt, then I feel justified in committing myself unreservedly to his defense."

"And if you can't believe him to be innocent?"

"Then I decline the case." A sigh escaped the lawyer's lips. "Your husband admitted his guilt. He seemed quite unrepentant, he asserted his moral right to act as he had done. And, because at the time I could see some justification for his behavior, I enlisted in his service." He set his jaw. "Perhaps it's just as well," he said, "that he declined to pay the fee upon which we'd agreed."

"He boasted about that, Martin."

How sweet his name sounded on those plump lips!

"Did he indeed."

"'I gave him a tenth of what he wanted,' he said, 'and he was lucky to get anything at all from me.' Of course he wasn't just bragging, he was letting me know just how tightfisted I could expect him to be."

"Yes, he'd have that in mind."

"You asked if I'd shown the pre-nup to an attorney. I had trouble finding one who'd look at it, or even let me into his office. What I discovered was that Millard had consulted every matrimonial lawyer within a radius of five hundred miles. He'd had each of them review the agreement and spend five minutes discussing it with him, and as a result they were ethically enjoined from representing me."

"For perhaps a thousand dollars a man, he'd made it impossible for you to secure representation." Ehrengraf frowned. "He did all this after discovering about you and young Bogue?"

"He began these consultations when we returned from our honeymoon."

"Had your discontent already become evident?"

"Not even to me, Martin. Millard was simply taking precautions." She finished her Drambuie, set down the empty glass. "And I did find a lawyer, a young man with a general practice, who took a look at the agreement I'd signed. He kept telling me it wasn't his area of expertise. But he said it looked rock-solid to him."

"Ah," said Ehrengraf. "Well, we'll have to see about that, won't we?"

≡

It was three weeks and a day later when Ehrengraf emerged from his morning shower and toweled himself dry. He shaved, and spent a moment or two trimming a few errant hairs from his beard, a Van Dyke that came to a precise point.

Beards had come and go in Ehrengraf's life, and upon his chin, and he felt this latest incarnation was the most successful to date. There was just the least hint of gray in it, even as there was the slightest touch of gray at his temples.

He hoped it would stay that way, at least for a while. With gray, as with so many things, a little was an asset, a lot a liability. Nor could one successfully command time to stand still, any more than King Canute could order a cessation of the tidal flow. There would be more gray, and the day would come when he would either accept it (and, by implication, all the slings and arrows of the aging process) or reach for the bottle of hair coloring.

Neither prospect was appealing. But both were off in the future, and did not bear thinking about. Certainly not on what was to be a day of triumph, a triumph all the sweeter for having been delayed.

He took his time dressing, choosing his newest suit, a three-piece navy pinstripe from Peller & Mure. He considered several shirts and settled on a spread-collar broadcloth in French blue, not least of all for the way it would complement his tie.

And the choice of tie was foreordained. It was, of course, that of the Caedmon Society.

The spread collar called for a Double Windsor, and Ehrengraf's fingers were equal to the task. He slipped his feet into black monk-strap loafers, then considered the suit's third piece, the vest. The only argument against it was that it would conceal much of his tie, but the tie and its significance were important only to the wearer.

He decided to go with the vest.

And now? It was getting on for nine, and his appointment was at his office, at half-past ten. He'd had his light breakfast, and the day was clear and bright and neither too warm nor too cold. He could walk to his office, taking his time, stopping along the way for a cup of coffee.

But why not wait and see if the phone might chance to ring?

And it did, just after nine o'clock. Ehrengraf smiled when it rang, and his smile broadened at the sound of the caller's voice, and broadened further as he listened. "Yes, of course," he said. "I'd like that."

"When we spoke yesterday," Alicia Ravenstock said, "I automatically suggested a meeting at your office. Because I'd been uncomfortable going there before, and now the reason for that discomfort had been removed."

"So you wanted to exercise your new freedom."

"Then I remembered what a nice apartment you have, and what good coffee I enjoyed on my previous visit."

"When you called," Ehrengraf said, "the first thing I did was make a fresh pot."

He fetched a cup for each of them, and watched her purse her lips and take a first sip.

"Just right," she said. "There's so much to talk about, Martin, but I'd like to get the business part out of the way."

She drew an envelope from her purse, and Ehrengraf held his breath, at least metaphorically, while he opened it. This was the second time he'd received an envelope from someone with Ravenstock for a surname, and the first time had proved profoundly disappointing.

Still, she'd used his first name, and moved their meeting from his office to his residence. Those ought to be favorable omens.

The check, he saw at a glance, had the correct number of zeroes. His eyes widened when he took a second look at it.

"This is higher than the sum we agreed on," he said.

"By ten percent. I've suddenly become a wealthy woman, Martin, and I felt a bonus was in order. I hope you don't regard it as an insult—"

Money? An insult? He assured her that it was nothing of the sort.

"It's really quite remarkable," she said. "Millard is in jail, where he's being held without bail. I've filed suit for divorce, and my attorney assures me that the pre-nup is essentially null and void. Martin, I knew the evidence against Bo was bogus. But I had no idea it would all come to light as it has."

"It was an interesting chain of events," he agreed.

"It was a tissue of lies," she said, "and it started to unravel when someone called Channel Seven's investigative reporter, pointing out that Bo was at a hockey game when the Milf Murder took place. How could he be in two places at the same time?"

"How indeed?"

"And then there was the damning physical evidence, the lacrosse shirt with Bo's DNA. They found a receipt among the boy's effects for a bag of clothes donated to Goodwill Industries, and among the several items mentioned was one Nichols School lacrosse jersey. How Millard knew about the donation and got his hands on the shirt—"

"We may never know, Alicia. And it may not have been Millard himself who found the shirt."

"It was probably Bainbridge. But we won't know that, either, now that he's dead."

"Suicide is a terrible thing," Ehrengraf said. "And sometimes it seems to ask as many questions as it answers. Though this particular act did answer quite a few."

"Walter Bainbridge was Millard's closest friend in the police department, and I thought it was awfully convenient the way he came up with all the evidence against Bo. But I guess Channel Seven's investigation convinced him he'd gone too far, and when the truth about the lacrosse shirt came to light, he could see the walls closing in. How desperate he must have been to put his service revolver in his mouth and blow his brains out."

"It was more than the evidence he faked. The note he left suggests he himself may have committed the Milf Murder. You see, it's almost certain he committed a similar rape and murder in Kenmore just days before he took his own life."

"The nurse," she remembered. "There was no physical evidence at the crime scene, but his note alluded to 'other bad things I've done,' and didn't they find something of hers in Bainbridge's desk at police headquarters?"

"A pair of soiled panties."

"The pervert. So he had ample reason to pin the Milf Murder on Bo. To help Millard, and to divert any possible suspicion from himself. This really is superb coffee."

"May I bring you a fresh cup?"

"Not quite yet, Martin. Those notebooks of Bo's, with the crude drawings and the fantasies? They seemed so unlikely to me, so much at variance with the Tegrum Bogue I knew, and well they might have done."

"They've turned out to be forgeries."

"Rather skillful forgeries," she said, "but forgeries all the same. Bainbridge had imitated Bo's handwriting, and he'd left behind a notebook in which he'd written out drafts of the material in his own hand, then practiced copying them in Bo's. And do you know what else they found?"

"Something of your husband's, I believe."

"Millard supplied those fantasies for Bainbridge. He wrote them out in his own cramped hand, and gave them to Bainbridge to save his policeman friend the necessity of using his imagination. But before he did this he made photocopies, which he kept. They turned up in a strongbox in his closet, and they were a perfect match for the originals that had been among Bainbridge's effects."

"Desperate men do desperate things," he said. "I'm sure he denies everything."

"Of course. It won't do him any good. The police came out of this looking very bad, and it's no help to blame Walter Bainbridge, as he's beyond their punishment. So they blame Millard for everything Bainbridge did, and for tempting Bainbridge in the first place. They were quite rough with him when they arrested him. You know how on television they always put a hand on a perpetrator's head when they're helping him get into the back seat of the squad car?"

"So that he won't bump his head on the roof."

"Well, this police detective put his hand on Millard's head," she said, "and then slammed it into the roof."

"I've often wondered if that ever happens."

"I saw it happen, Martin. The policeman said he was sorry."

"It must have been an accident."

"Then he did it again."

"Oh."

"I wish I had a tape of it," she said. "I'd watch it over and over."

The woman had heart, Ehrengraf marveled. Her beauty was exceptional, but ultimately it was merely a component of a truly remarkable spirit. He could think of things to say, but he was content for now to leave them unsaid, content merely to bask in the glow of her presence.

And Alicia seemed comfortable with the silence. Their eyes met, and it seemed to Ehrengraf that their breathing took on the same cadence, deepening their wordless intimacy.

"You don't want more coffee," he said at length.

She shook her head.

"The last time you were here—"

"You gave me a Drambuie."

"Would you like one now?"

"Not just now. Do you know what I almost suggested last time?"

He did not.

"It was after you'd brought me the Drambuie, but before I'd tasted it. The thought came to me that we should go to your bedroom and make love, and afterward we could drink the Drambuie."

"But you didn't."

"No. I knew you wanted me, I could tell by the way you looked at me."

"I didn't mean to stare."

"I didn't find it objectionable, Martin. It wasn't a coarse or lecherous look. It was admiring. I found it exciting."

"I see."

"Add in the fact that you're a very attractive man, Martin, and one in whose presence I feel safe and secure, and, well, I found myself overcome by a very strong desire to go to bed with you."

"My dear lady."

"But the timing was wrong," she said. "And how would you take it? Might it seem like a harlot's trick to bind you more strongly to my service? So the moment came and went, and we drained our little snifters of Drambuie, and I went home to Nottingham Terrace."

Ehrengraf waited.

"Now everything's resolved," she said. "I wanted to give you the check first thing, so that would be out of the way. And we've said what we needed to say about my awful husband and that wretched policeman. And I find I want you more than ever. And you still want me, don't you, Martin?"

"More than ever."

"Afterward," she said, "we'll have the Drambuie."

The EHRENGRAF Fandango

"Let this be said between us here,
One love grows green when one turns grey;
This year knows nothing of last year;
To-morrow has no more to say
To yesterday."
—Algernon Charles Swinburne

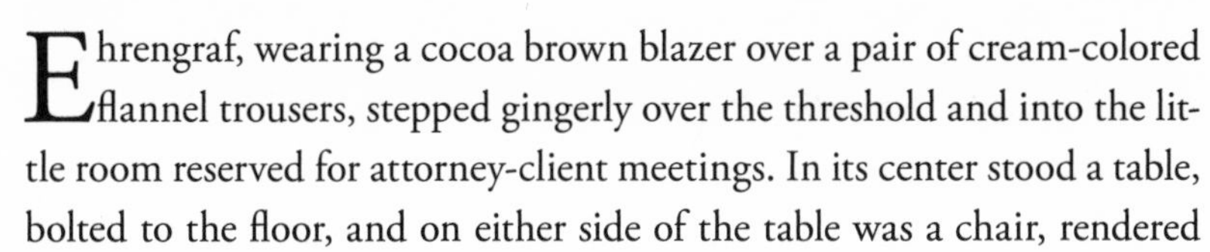

Ehrengraf, wearing a cocoa brown blazer over a pair of cream-colored flannel trousers, stepped gingerly over the threshold and into the little room reserved for attorney-client meetings. In its center stood a table, bolted to the floor, and on either side of the table was a chair, rendered immobile in the same fashion.

A young woman occupied one of the chairs and looked up at the little lawyer's approach. She was tall and slender, with nut-brown hair framing an oval face that would have delighted Modigliani. Mentally, Ehrengraf supplied her with the color and sparkle of which recent events had deprived her. He could tell that she'd be a beauty.

"Mr. Ehrengraf," she said.

"Ms. Plumley."

"Can we talk here?"

"That's the room's purpose," Ehrengraf said. "It's supposed to be preferable to meeting in a cell."

"And I suppose it is. But can what we say be heard?"

"I wouldn't worry about it," he said.

Which, he thought, was accurate, if not entirely responsive. Sitting in that room, breathing its stale air, Ehrengraf recalled a very different room, one he'd encountered a few years ago when business had called him to New York. There, a pebble's throw from Carnegie Hall, he dined in a restaurant with an interior designed by the artist Milton Glaser. He recalled patterned tile rugs set into the tiled floor, but more than that he remembered the motif of super-sized representations of the human anatomy, sculpted and hanging on the walls. Here a disembodied nose, there a pair of sculpted lips. And, most memorably, an enormous ear.

The room's décor was as over-the-top as this room's was austere, even non-existent. But Ehrengraf imagined its walls covered with ears, thousands of ears, big ears and little ears, all of them listening, for what else did ears do?

But he wouldn't worry about it.

"Actually," Cheryl Plumley said, "there's no reason for me to worry about it. Everyone knows I did it."

Responses sprang up in Ehrengraf's mind and dematerialized before they reached his lips. He waited.

"That's why I insisted they call you," she went on. "'You have the right to remain silent. You have the right to an attorney.' I felt as though I was in a crime show on television. Reading me my rights. I mean, I was ready to change my name to Miranda."

"You were right to call me."

"Oh, I knew that was the thing to do. I don't remember who it was I heard it from, but I've never forgotten. 'If you ever kill somebody, if you're guilty as sin, the man to call is Martin H. Ehrengraf.'"

"Indeed," said Ehrengraf, and sighed a small sigh. "It pains me to hear you say that," he said, "because it could not be further from the truth. My role, Ms. Plumley, is that of defender of the innocent. I have never represented a guilty client."

Her face, already jailhouse pale, nevertheless managed to lose color. "Then I've made a mistake," she said.

"Not at all."

"Because if you only represent innocent people—"

"As indeed I do."

"—then you can't represent me, can you?"

"Why ever not?"

"Because I'm guilty. Why are you shaking your head?"

"Because I don't agree. Ms. Plumley, my dear Ms. Plumley, I know you to be innocent."

"Innocent," said Cheryl Plumley. "I just learned how much I want to believe that. When you said what you said, when I heard those words, a surge of emotion shot through me. And now I don't know whether to laugh or cry."

"If you're not certain," Ehrengraf said, "it's probably best to do neither. I'll say it again, dear lady. I know you to be innocent."

"How can you? The whole world knows me to be guilty. And yet—"

"Yes?"

"Even though I did it, even though I fired the pistol that killed those people, I could argue that I wasn't truly responsible for what happened in that house on Woodbridge Avenue. It wouldn't make any difference in a court of law, and I'm not sure I really believe it myself. But it's an argument I could make."

"Then make it."

She lowered her eyes, then raised them almost defiantly. "Very well," she said. "The Devil made me do it."

"Believe me," Cheryl Plumley said, "I know how that sounds. You must think I'm barking mad."

Neither barking nor mad, Ehrengraf thought. But possessed of an interesting turn of mind, certainly, and one which presented possibilities.

"I don't even believe in the Devil," she went on. "At least I don't think I do."

"Unlike the Deity," Ehrengraf said, "the Devil doesn't seem to require that one believe in him. One can but wonder why. But let's put that question aside for the moment, shall we? And why don't you tell me what happened?"

"I don't remember everything. I suppose that's evidence of guilt in and of itself, wouldn't you say? My guilty conscience must have erased the memory."

That struck Ehrengraf as rather more of a stretch than believing in the Devil, or even the Tooth Fairy.

"I don't know where to begin, Mr. Ehrengraf. I woke up that morning, I prepared my own breakfast, I watched a news program on television. I left my house around ten-thirty and drove to my gym, where I took a yoga class from eleven to twelve. I had lunch with a friend at the Hour Glass, and she told me about a shop on Englewood with a good selection of ceramic tiles imported from Italy. I've been thinking about doing some renovation and, well, I thought it would be good to see what they had."

"So you drove there?"

"I must have."

"But you don't remember?"

She shook her head. "I remember leaving the restaurant," she said, "and I remember getting in my car, and then everything's just gone."

"Gone."

"The slate wiped clean. The next thing I knew—"

"Yes?"

"I was in that house."

"The Kuhldreyer home."

"Yes, but I didn't know it at the time. I must have driven past that house dozens of times, it's right there on Woodbridge between Starin and Voorhees, but I'd never paid any particular attention to it."

"And you didn't know the Kuhldreyers."

"I knew her in high school. Knew who she was, anyway. I don't think we ever had an actual conversation."

"Mrs. Kuhldreyer."

"Not at the time. She was Mary Beth Dooley, and she was two years behind me at Bennett, and she giggled."

"She giggled."

"A lot of girls do," she said, "at that age. That's about as much as I ever knew about her, and then all of a sudden I was in her house, and I had a gun in my hand." She looked at her hand, as if it still held the weapon. "It was very heavy," she said.

"The gun."

"Yes. It was in my hand, and my finger was on the trigger, and they were all dead."

"And did you know who they were?"

She shook her head. "I didn't recognize her," she said. "Mary Beth. I barely knew her in high school and hadn't seen her since. And I'd never met him."

"Richard Kuhldreyer."

"He was lying on the rug in front of the fireplace," she said. "I guess he was standing when I shot him, and he fell down there. She was on the sofa, it was one of those Victorian love seats, and I'd shot her once in the face and once in the chest. And then there was another woman."

"Patricia Munk."

"Another person I'd never heard of until I killed her with a single shot to the head. She lived across the street from the Kuhldreyers, and I don't know what she was doing at their house that afternoon."

Keeping an appointment in Samarra, Ehrengraf supposed.

"Before the event," he said, "the last thing you remember is getting in your car."

"Yes."

"And then the next thing you recall—"

"Is standing in their living room with a gun in my hand."

"A gun which you'd already fired."

"Yes, although I have no recollection of firing it."

"And the people in the room—"

"Are lying there dead. I'm seeing them for the first time, and they're dead, because I've killed them."

"By pointing the gun in your hand and pulling the trigger, but you don't remember so doing."

"No, but who else could have done it? I was all alone in the room. Except for three people who could hardly have done it, because they were all dead."

Ehrengraf thought it over, and made a little tent of his fingers. Or might it better be a church? He extended both index fingers, interlaced the others. Here's the church, here's the steeple, open the doors and see all the people—

"Lunch," he said.

"I beg your pardon?"

"You had lunch," he said. "At the Hour Glass, with a friend."

"Yes."

"What did you have to eat?"

"What did I have to eat? Why on earth is that important?"

"What might be important," he said, "is your recollection of it."

"Fish," she said. "Filet of sole almandine. With a green salad. I had the house dressing on the salad."

"And your companion," Ehrengraf said.

"I don't remember what she had. Maybe if I concentrate—"

"I don't care what she had. Tell me about her."

"Hypnotized," Cheryl Plumley said.

Ehrengraf marked his place in a book of Swinburne's verse and regarded his client, who sat in the red leather chair to the side of his chronically untidy desk. At their initial meeting the little lawyer had sensed the beauty damped down by imprisonment. Now, her anxiety dispelled with the restoration of her freedom, the woman positively glowed.

"Barring Satanic intervention," Ehrengraf said, "no other explanation came to mind. You had acted in an uncharacteristic manner, taking the lives of a man and two women, for no discernible reason, and with no recollection of having done so. What more obvious explanation than that you had been hypnotized?"

"By Maureen McClintock."

"The woman with whom you'd lunched at the Hour Glass. Not a close friend, merely a casual acquaintance—and yet after an hour in her company, you'd returned abruptly to consciousness in a strange house with a smoking gun in your hand."

"I thought I must have fired it. And killed those people."

"A natural conclusion, to be sure. There you were, after all, gun in hand. And there they were, shot dead. Hypnosis, as I understand it, can't lead one to commit an act against one's nature. I could not hypnotize you and compel you to beat your infant son to death with a tire iron."

"I don't have a son."

"Or a tire iron, Ms. Plumley, but that's neither here nor there. Supposing you had both, hypnosis would not lead you to use one upon the other. But if you were encouraged to believe that the tire iron was in fact a fly swatter, and the child a pesky mosquito—"

"Oh. And that's what happened in the house on Woodbridge Avenue?"

Ehrengraf shook his head. "Not at all," he said. "They never gave you a paraffin test."

"A paraffin test?"

"To detect nitrate particles on your skin, a natural consequence of firing a gun. It's routinely performed in such cases, when someone is suspected of firing a gun, but they didn't bother in your case because it seemed superfluous. There you were with the gun in your hand, and they assumed you'd fired it, and you didn't deny it."

"Because I didn't remember." She brightened. "But if they didn't do the test, that meant I didn't fire the gun!"

It meant no such thing, Ehrengraf knew, but he let it go.

"If you didn't," he said, "then someone else did. And even if you had in fact gunned those people down, you could only have done so under the impression that they were flies and the handgun was a fly swatter."

"How could I think—"

"Oh, not literally," he said, and fingered the knot in his tie. It was his Caedmon Society necktie, his usual choice for moments of triumph, and was this not a triumphant occasion? Had he not once again snatched an innocent client from the jaws of what the media persistently called the criminal justice system?

"But—"

"Perhaps the suggestion implanted under hypnosis was that you were playing a violent video game, and that Patricia Munk and the Kuhldreyers were images on an Xbox screen; by zapping them with your ray gun, you'd advance to the next level of the game."

"I've never played a video game."

"Nor did you play this one," Ehrengraf said smoothly, "because in fact you didn't shoot anyone. It was Maureen McClintock who did the shooting, then pressed the gun into your hand and slipped out the door. Perhaps she told you that you'd wake up when you heard a doorbell, and rang it just before getting into her car and driving away. You heard it, you returned to full consciousness, and what else were you to believe but that you'd caused the mayhem before you?"

"So you were right, Mr. Ehrengraf. I really was innocent. But the police—"

"Did everything one might have hoped for, once they were steered in the right direction. They'd never had reason to take a good look at Maureen McClintock, whose connection to the matter seemed limited to her having shared a table with you earlier. But once they did, they found no end of evidence to implicate her and exonerate you."

"She'd studied hypnotism."

"She owned over a dozen books on the subject," he said, "all of them well-thumbed, along with a fifteen-lesson correspondence course. And they weren't out on display where anyone might have noticed them. They were tucked away out of sight, as if she didn't want anyone to know of her interest in the subject."

"Which she denied, according to the papers."

"Stoutly," said Ehrengraf. "Maintained she'd never seen them before in her life."

"Then how did she explain them?"

"She couldn't. She also maintained she'd never had any contact with the Kuhldreyers, or with Patricia Munk. And yet there was a newspaper clipping, news of a promotion Mr. Kuhldreyer had received. And a photograph of the couple, and a rather startling letter from Patricia Munk."

"I read as much in the paper. But they didn't go into detail."

"They couldn't," Ehrengraf said. "It was quite graphic in nature. Evidently Munk and McClintock had had an affair, and Munk wrote about it at some length, and in some detail. You couldn't reproduce it in a family newspaper."

"I didn't know Maureen well," Cheryl Plumley said, "but I had no idea she was gay."

"Something else she denies, but her denial is severely compromised, not only by Munk's letter to her but by several letters she seems to have written to Munk, found in a hat box in the dead woman's closet. Of course she swears she never wrote those letters. Oh, it's a sad case indeed, Ms. Plumley. What did she have against the Kuhldreyers? Was it some sort of love triangle, or quadrangle? And why choose you as a cat's-paw for her adventure in triple homicide?"

"So many questions, Mr. Ehrengraf, and I can't answer any of them. But I'll have to, won't I?"

"Oh?"

"For the book."

"Ah, the book," said Ehrengraf, and drew a document of several pages from a manila folder. "I've looked this over, Ms. Plumley, and I believe it's ready for your signature. The publisher has agreed to improve his terms, and they're now quite generous. You'll work with an accomplished author, a very talented and personable young woman named Nan Fassbinder, and I'll vet the final document to make sure the words she puts in your mouth are acceptable. Now if you could sign your name here, Cheryl Jonellen Plumley, that's right, and here, and here as well. And now you'll be able to tell your story to the world."

"The part I remember," she said, "which isn't very much at all, but the wonderful part is that now I'll be able to pay your fee. I was worried about that, you know, but you told me not to worry, and I had a thought that, well, it seems embarrassing now. I don't know if I should mention it."

In Ehrengraf's experience, a mere pause was often all it took to prompt a fuller explanation. Such was the case now.

"What struck me on our first meeting," Cheryl Plumley said, "was what an attractive man you are. When you told me I was innocent, I quivered with a sensation that was more than mere relief. And then, when you rescued me from what looked to be an absolutely hopeless situation, I was overcome by the desire to express my gratitude in, um—"

"Physical form?"

"Yes. But to do so when I was unable to pay your fee, well, that wouldn't be proper, would it? It would look as though, well, you know how it would look."

"Yes."

"But now, with the book deal taking care of your compensation, and, oh, this is so awkward, Mr. Ehrengraf, but—"

"My dear Ms. Plumley," Ehrengraf said, and took her hand, and brushed it with his lips. What a sweet little hand it was, so soft, with tapering fingers. "I do believe," he said, "that we'd be more comfortable on the sofa."

Ehrengraf had just finished knotting his Caedmon Society necktie when his client returned from the lavatory. She was nicely dressed once again, after having been ever so nicely undressed. He looked at her, and his gaze brought a blush to her cheeks even as it put a smile on her lips.

"I feel quite wonderful," she said. "Everything's worked out perfectly, hasn't it?"

"It has."

"For everyone but Maureen McClintock," Cheryl Plumley said. "I don't suppose I should sympathize with her, after what she did to those people and what she tried to do to me. But I was locked up myself until very recently, and I know how awful that is."

"Indeed."

"And while I never knew her terribly well, she always seemed like such a nice person. I ask myself how she could have done what she did, and the answer that pops into my head—well, you'll just think it's silly."

"Oh?"

"Maybe the Devil made her do it," she said. "But that's perfectly ridiculous, isn't it?"

═══

"Perfectly ridiculous," said Maureen McClintock. "As I didn't *do* any of the things with which I'm charged, there's nothing for the Devil to have made me do."

"I know," Ehrengraf said.

"I'm supposed to be the worst woman since Lucrezia Borgia," she said, "with the possible exception of that woman who drowned her two little boys, and she at least was clearly demented. Is that how you propose to save me? Because I'm not crazy."

"I know."

"Though how can I be sure? 'I'm not crazy' is, after all, one of the things crazy people say. And what's the point of saying it? The people who already know you're sane don't require reassurance, and the others won't find your proclamation convincing." She frowned. "One can almost see the Devil's hand in it, can't one? Because the whole affair is truly diabolical. All the evidence in the world points to my guilt as a multiple murderess. And yet I'm innocent."

"I know."

She looked at him, as if seeing him for the first time. Ehrengraf, his usual natty self in a gray flannel suit, a French blue shirt, and a navy tie, took the opportunity to look at his new client, and liked what he saw. Her drab outfit notwithstanding, she was a fine-looking woman, and he could see strength and purpose in her facial features.

His recent experience in his office provided him with an interesting image—Maureen McClintock, divested of her garments, stretched out upon his brown leather sofa.

All in due time, he told himself.

"'I know,'" she echoed him. "You keep saying that, Mr. Ehrengraf."

"I suppose I do."

"I said I was innocent, and you said, 'I know.'"

"I did."

"Were you acknowledging my remark? As if nodding to keep the conversation moving?"

He shook his head. "I was acknowledging your innocence. Because I know you didn't kill anybody, my dear Ms. McClintock, nor did you persuade anyone else to do so, through hypnotism or another of the dark arts. You were artfully—one might even say diabolically—framed, by someone whose intent was to commit murder and get away with it."

"Cheryl Plumley."

"Certainly not," said Ehrengraf. "Ms. Plumley was my client."

"But—"

"And my clients are innocent, Ms. McClintock. I did not endure the tedium of law school or brave the rigors of the bar exam in order to serve as cupbearer to the guilty. I represent—gladly, proudly—the innocent."

"You're saying that Cheryl and I are both innocent."

"I am."

"And someone else—"

"Framed you both, so arranging matters that Ms. Plumley appeared to have committed the murder while you appeared to have hovered in the background pulling the strings. Those books on hypnotism, Ms. McClintock. Did you buy them? Study them in detail?"

"I never even laid eyes on them," she said, "until the police searched my home and pointed them out to me." She frowned at a memory. "I *was* hypnotized once," she remembered, "if that's what it was. I wanted to lose a few pounds, and a friend had gone to a hypnotherapist, and she said it helped. So I went, and I guess he hypnotized me, but I can't say I felt any different afterward. I picked up a pint of ice cream on the way home."

"So it didn't work."

"Well, maybe it did," she said, "because two weeks later I joined a gym and booked sessions with a personal trainer, and *that* worked. Maybe that man put me in a trance and told me to join a gym." She straightened in her chair. "I didn't buy those books, I didn't hypnotize Cheryl, I didn't do any of those things."

"You don't have to tell me that, Ms. McClintock."

"But how can you prove it in court?"

"I am rarely called upon to prove anything in court, Ms. McClintock. I find courtrooms airless and joyless venues, and make a point of staying out of them. What I intend to do, my dear woman, is so arrange matters that the facts of the case become known. When that happens, the innocence which is now so obvious to me will become evident to one and all."

And toward that end, he told her, he'd need to know something about her life and the people in it.

"Whitley Pleskow," Maureen McClintock said, on their next meeting. "Why, I can barely picture what he looks like. It's been years since I saw him, and our relationship never amounted to much of anything. I'm not even sure you can call it a relationship. We had a couple of dates, and I should have ended it at that point because I knew the chemistry wasn't there."

"But you didn't."

"No, and the next time I saw him I went to bed with him, and that confirmed what I'd already realized."

"The lack of chemistry."

"And when it's not there, it's never going to be there, is it? But that's not knowledge one is born with. You have to learn it, and Whit was part of my education. I saw him a few more times, and we went to bed, and I guess he liked it enough to want to keep on seeing me, but I didn't."

"And you broke it off."

"In a pleasant and painless way," she said, "or at least that's what I always thought. But I guess it wasn't that pleasant or painless for him."

Ehrengraf fingered the knot in his Caedmon Society necktie. "Swinburne," he said.

"Swinburne?"

"The nineteenth century British poet, Ms. McClintock. 'One love grows green when one turns grey.' But it seems to have been Mr. Pleskow who turned green."

"With jealousy?"

"Or envy," he said, "or something of the sort. To all appearances, Mr. Pleskow went on with his life. He dated other women, and eventually he married one of them. The marriage failed, and again he went on with his life. And yet, throughout it all, he remained fixated on one woman. And that would be you, Ms. McClintock."

She shuddered. "It seems impossible," she said. "And yet I saw that photograph."

"The little shrine. Photographs of you, and newspaper clippings. A little altar, on which he'd burned black candles."

"What does it mean, burning a black candle?"

"It can't mean anything good," Ehrengraf said. "He was entirely obsessed with you. The police found notebooks filled with letters he wrote to you but never sent. They found little stories of his. Fantasies, really, in which you were a principal player."

"I read about them."

"But the press couldn't reproduce them, because they were relentlessly obscene. And violent as well—in some of his writings you were abused and tortured and murdered, while in others you were the villain, having your way with men or women and dispatching them horribly once you were done with them."

"How awful."

"In one particularly inventive episode," Ehrengraf recalled, "you and Cheryl Plumley were lesbian lovers, and the two of you impaled a young woman upon a sharpened stake and made love while she slowly bled to death. Your victim is referred to only as Patsy, but her description is that of poor Patricia Munk."

"I never had any idea. I'd forgotten him, and I assumed he'd forgotten me. It's harrowing to think I could have played that sort of unwitting role in his personal mythology." She drew a breath. "I guess we'll never know how he managed to do what he did. Putting Cheryl in the Kuhldreyer house, planting incriminating material in my home. It's amazing he worked it all out, let alone carried it off."

"It's unfortunate," Ehrengraf said, "that he's not able to give an account of his actions. It pains me to say it, but I blame myself."

"You? But why, Mr. Ehrengraf?"

"When my investigations began to bear fruit," he said, "I should have gone straight to the police. But one hesitates to do so while the possibility of innocence still exists. And so I'm afraid I had a conversation with Mr. Pleskow. I hoped to secure information without divulging any myself, but I fear I left him aware that he was under suspicion. And thus, after I left him—"

"He took the easy way out."

Easy, thought Ehrengraf, may not have been the most appropriate word for Whitley Pleskow's fitful little dance at the end of a rope. But he let it go.

"In a sense," Ehrengraf said, "he may be said to have done us a favor. Some unscrupulous defense attorney could have turned the courtroom into a circus arena. Why, for all we know Pleskow could have fabricated an alibi, could have chipped away at the mountain of evidence against him. But his final act, bolstered by a suicide note in his own hand, removes all doubt. While we may never know precisely how he brought it off, we can be certain that the triple homicide on Woodbridge Avenue was his work and his work alone. Cheryl Plumley is entirely innocent. And so, my dear Ms. McClintock, are you."

Her hand fastened on his arm. "Mr. Ehrengraf," she said, not quite purring. "I don't know how to thank you."

Ehrengraf, waiting for his client to return from the lavatory, tried to remember what he'd paid for the leather sofa. Whatever the price, it had been money well spent. And it seemed to him that the piece of furniture improved with use, as if it were seasoned like a fine meerschaum pipe by the sport conducted upon it.

"That was lovely," Maureen McClintock said upon her return. "But I still owe you a fee, and I'm sure it must be a substantial one, because you deserve no less."

Ehrengraf named a figure.

The woman's face fell. "It's about what I expected," she said, "and I'd write a check for the full amount, and even tag on a bonus. But—"

"But you're in no position to do so."

"I'm solvent," she said, "and I've always been able to meet my expenses. But I've never been able to put money aside, and I don't have any reserves to draw upon."

"Ah," said Ehrengraf. "My dear Ms. McClintock, you have an asset of which you may not be aware."

"Oh?"

"You have a story, Ms. McClintock. A very valuable story. And I'm acquainted with a woman who can help you share it with the world."

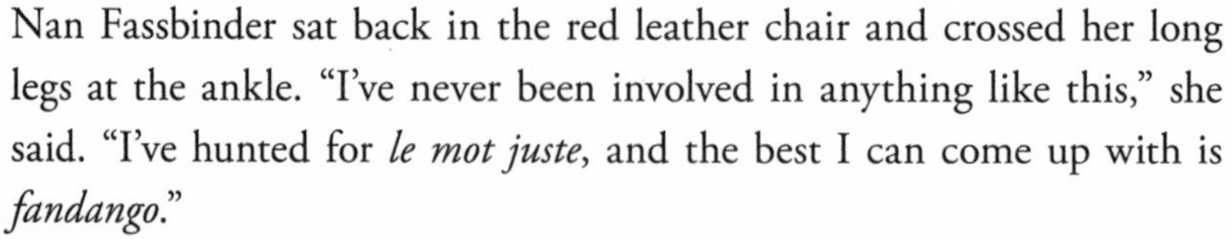

Nan Fassbinder sat back in the red leather chair and crossed her long legs at the ankle. "I've never been involved in anything like this," she said. "I've hunted for *le mot juste*, and the best I can come up with is *fandango*."

"Isn't that a dance?"

"A Spanish dance," she said. "Figuratively, it has several meanings. According to Wikipedia, where I looked it up just hours ago, it may mean a quarrel, a big fuss, or a brilliant exploit."

"And when you use it now—"

"A brilliant exploit, of course. I'm in awe."

"Well," said Ehrengraf.

"I'm also hugely grateful," she said. "I have to thank you for Cheryl Plumley and Maureen McClintock. The publisher's over the moon, you know. Two women, both of them wonderfully articulate and deliciously attractive, and each with a gripping story to tell. And of course the two stories reinforce one another, and anyone who reads one of the books is impelled to reach for the other."

"Which can only be good for all concerned."

"Good for the publisher, who'll sell a ton of books. Good for Cheryl and Maureen, both of whom are getting media coaching even as we speak. They're competitive, but in a good way, and they can't wait to chase separately around the country on their book tours, with a few joint appearances in major cities as a highlight."

"I suspect they'll be good at it."

"No kidding," Nan Fassbinder said. "So it'll be good for them, and I guess it'll be good for you, because the advances they got enabled them to pay for your services."

"Almost beside the point," Ehrengraf said. "Still, one does like to be adequately compensated for one's efforts."

"And good for me, Martin. May I call you Martin?"

"Of course, my dear Nan."

"Good for me, because I'll do very well as the co-author of both of these books, and if they're as successful as I think they'll be, it'll boost my stock for future projects. You might say I owe you a debt of gratitude, Martin."

"No more than the one I owe you, Nan."

"Hmmm," she said. "You know, both of those women speak very highly of you, Martin. And I got the definite impression that it was more than your legal acumen that they appreciated."

"Oh?"

"That sofa," Nan Fassbinder said. "Can it possibly be as comfortable as it looks?"

AFTERWORD

In 1978, Ellery Queen's Mystery Magazine *published "The Ehrengraf Defense," the debut appearance of the dapper little lawyer who never loses a case. In 1994, Jim Seels published a deluxe small-press edition of the eight Ehrengraf stories. Edward D. Hoch, surely the reigning contemporary master of short crime fiction, provided the following introduction:*

When Lawrence Block asked me to prepare this introduction to his eight stories about criminal lawyer Martin H. Ehrengraf, I'm sure he was unaware how ironic the request was. Back in the early 1950s, when I was still struggling to make my first sale, I began corresponding with Ben Abramson, a bookseller and Sherlockian who had previously published *The Baker Street Journal.* I even met with him on one of my trips to New York.

Abramson had discussed with Fred Dannay (the half of "Ellery Queen" who was actively editing *Ellery Queen's Mystery Magazine*) an idea for a series of stories about a criminal lawyer, in both senses of the phrase. This lawyer, patterned after the character of Randolph Mason created in 1896 by Melville Davisson Post, would be an unscrupulous attorney using the weaknesses of the law to defeat justice. Dannay was eager to run such a series, and suggested that Abramson seek out some young writer to tackle the project.

I had never read any of the Randolph Mason stories, but armed with a couple of plot suggestions from Ben Abramson I hurried home to write the first story. I sent the finished product off to Abramson and he liked it. Fred Dannay didn't, and the project quickly died.

A quarter of a century later Lawrence Block wrote a story about a criminal lawyer named Martin H. Ehrengraf and submitted it to

EQMM. "The Ehrengraf Method" (later reprinted as "The Ehrengraf Defense") was published in the February 1978 issue of the magazine, with a headnote by Dannay which spoke of filling the footprints of Post's Randolph Mason. Like me, Block had never read the Mason tales, but with the encouragement of Fred Dannay the new series lasted through eight stories, all but one of which appeared in *EQMM*. ("The Ehrengraf Appointment" didn't quite catch Dannay's favor, apparently, and found a home in *Mike Shayne Mystery Magazine*.)

What was there about Martin Ehrengraf, and Randolph Mason before him, that so fascinated readers? Perhaps it was the idea of outwitting the law, of finding some clever way around the firm structures of our legal system. In the first and best of the Mason books, *The Strange Schemes of Randolph Mason* (1896), the title character usually springs his surprises in the courtroom, baffling judge and jury alike as murderers, forgers and embezzlers walk free. Ehrengraf, on the other hand, prefers that his cases never even come to trial, that the charges against his clients be dropped. Ehrengraf says, "I prefer to leave that to the Perry Masons of the world." In a later story he explains, "I'm always happiest when I can save my clients not merely from prison but from going to trial in the first place."

Of course Ehrengraf goes further than Randolph Mason ever did. If Mason might advise a client to commit murder, and then free him on a technicality, Ehrengraf actually commits murder himself to aid a client and collect his fee. As Francis M. Nevins has observed, "(Block's) protagonist serves clients not by taking advantage of glitches in the system but by breaking the law in whatever way will work." The fact that Ehrengraf's felonies usually occur offstage and are only inferred does little to lessen their effect.

Randolph Mason developed in later stories into a sort of moral champion, defending clients victimized by villains using the legal system. Block, in the introduction to his 1983 collection *Sometimes They Bite*, pretty much assures us that this won't happen to Ehrengraf. But the dapper little attorney does love poetry, quoting at times from William Blake, Andrew Marvell, Christopher Smart, Arthur O'Shaughnessy and others. Like Shelley he believes that "poets are the unacknowledged legislators of the universe." Once he even speaks of himself as a "corrector of destinies" using the title of the very book in which Randolph Mason completed his metamorphosis into a force for good.

There has been no new Ehrengraf story now for ten years. Perhaps the little attorney with the neat mustache and a liking for poetry really has gone over to the side of rectitude. But somehow I doubt it.

Lawrence Block was recently a recipient of the Grand Master award from the Mystery Writers of America, one of the youngest writers to be so honored. It is a well-deserved tribute to an author who has proven adept in creating memorable series characters in both the novel and short story forms. With the current popularity of both the Matthew Scudder and Bernie Rhodenbarr novels, along with the Keller short stories, I'm pleased to see that Ehrengraf hasn't been forgotten.

Edward D. Hoch
Rochester, NY, 1994

And here's my afterword to that volume:

Amazing what you find out. To think that Fred Dannay was once interested in a continuation of Melville Davisson Post's Randolph Mason stories! To think that Ed Hoch once undertook to provide it!

I of course had no idea. When I wrote the first Ehrengraf story in 1977, I didn't know anything more about Melville Davisson Post than his name. Fred Dannay was crazy about the story, and heralded Ehrengraf as a lineal descendant of Randolph Mason.

I didn't know what the hell he was talking about. And I may have been just a tiny bit sensitive on the subject. Because, while I hadn't pilfered any ideas from Post, the first Ehrengraf story was an example of what I've elsewhere called Creative Plagiarism.

I hadn't stolen the character. Ehrengraf was my own creation, sprung from my high forehead like Athena from the brow of Zeus. No, what I'd stolen was the plot itself.

And not from Melville Davisson Post, either. I'd lifted it from Fletcher Flora.

I don't remember the title of the story, or just where and when it appeared. I'd guess it was published in *Manhunt*, probably in the mid-to-late fifties. While the details of the story have long since left my memory, I recall that it concerned a good friend of the narrator, who was in jail, charged with murdering a young woman. The narrator, operating on the principle that greater love hath no man than to lay down someone else's life for a friend, gets his buddy off the hook by committing another murder or two with the identical MO. The friend, securely in jail at the time, has an unshakable alibi, and is thus off the hook for the first murder, which he did in fact commit.

I read the story, I liked the story, I forgot about the story, and years later I remembered it again and thought what a pleasure it would be to write that story. There was only one problem. Someone had already written it.

So I thought some more about it, and started poking it and probing it, looking for ways to change it. I decided that an artful attorney would make a good hero, and it struck me that he'd be particularly well motivated if he worked, as negligence lawyers do, upon a contingency basis. Martin Ehrengraf took shape at once, the minute I started writing the first paragraph. All his traits and mannerisms were somehow there from the beginning, as if he'd been waiting patiently for me to sit down and write about him.

I didn't intend him as a series character, but characters have frequently surprised me in this fashion over the years, and I don't think a month passed after I'd written the first Ehrengraf story before I found myself writing a second.

Fred Dannay was the first editor to see the first Ehrengraf story, and he snapped it up for *EQMM. He* wasn't surprised when there was a second story, and did indeed hail my little lawyer as the reincarnation of Randolph Mason, and went on buying the stories as they rolled out of my typewriter. He passed on one, "The Ehrengraf Appointment", finding it too gory for his taste. Rather than rewrite it for him, I sent it off to *Mike Shayne*, where I sold it for the price of a dinner, and not a great dinner, either. Fred bought the next one, and the one after that, and after his death in 1982 Eleanor Sullivan continued to take what Ehrengraf stories I managed to write.

But there haven't been all that many of them. Early on, Otto Penzler told me he'd like to publish a collection of the Ehrengraf stories as soon as I got enough of them written to fill a book. That sounded good to me.

It never happened.

Ehrengraf's problem, you see, is that he has a severely limited range. There haven't been that many story ideas that have worked for him. I haven't wanted to write the same story over and over, and have waited for variations to suggest themselves. There have thus far been only these eight which appear together now for the first time.

I can't tell you there'll never be another. I write these lines in May of 1994, the publication month of *The Burglar Who Traded Ted Williams*, Bernie Rhodenbarr's first book-length adventure in over a decade. If Bernie could come back after so long an absence, I can hardly rule out an eventual future appearance of the wily Martin Herod (or Harrod) Ehrengraf. I wouldn't hold my breath, but I'm not going to say it'll never happen.

For now, though—and perhaps forever—all the Ehrengraf stories are available in a single volume, arranged in the order in which they were written. I hope you like the dapper little fellow. I can tell you I had a good time writing about him.

Lawrence Block

Greenwich Village, 1994

≡

That was then and this is now, and twenty years have passed without Ehrengraf's having lost a step or a case. And I'm pleased to report that the reformation which sullied the latter days of Randolph Mason has not visited itself upon our little lawyer.

The story count for Ehrengraf now stands at twelve—the body count is of course a good deal higher—and it would please me if there should turn out to be more tales yet to be recounted. For now, though, it would seem that there are enough of them to warrant a new edition of the collected stories.

I hope you've enjoyed them. (Or, if you've cheated and read the afterword first, I hope such enjoyment lies in your future.)

It is my earnest wish for you, Gentle Reader, that you never have need of Ehrengraf's services. But life is an uncertain enterprise; should you find yourself in such desperate straits, I can but wish that you secure an advocate who will represent your interests with the zeal and dispatch of Martin H. Ehrengraf.

And, after he's worked his magic on your behalf, I trust you'll have the good sense to pay his fee. In full, and at once.

It would be the greatest folly to do otherwise…

Lawrence Block
Greenwich Village, 2014